The Dragon Recruit

Lochguard Highland Dragons
Book 11

Jessie Donovan

Mythical Lake Press, LLC

The Dragon Recruit

Copyright © 2025 Laura Hoak-Kagey

Mythical Lake Press, LLC

Print Edition

Cover Art by Laura Hoak-Kagey of Mythical Lake Design

ISBN: 979-8891560611

The Stonefire and Lochguard series intertwine with one another. (As well as with one Tahoe Dragon Mates book.) Since so many readers ask for the overall reading order, I've included it with this book. (This list is as of May 2025.)

Sacrificed to the Dragon (Stonefire Dragons #1)
Seducing the Dragon (Stonefire Dragons #2)
Revealing the Dragons (Stonefire Dragons #3)
Healed by the Dragon (Stonefire Dragons #4)
Reawakening the Dragon (Stonefire Dragons #5)
The Dragon's Dilemma (Lochguard Highland Dragons #1)
Loved by the Dragon (Stonefire Dragons #6)
The Dragon Guardian (Lochguard Highland Dragons #2)
Surrendering to the Dragon (Stonefire Dragons #7)
The Dragon's Heart (Lochguard Highland Dragons #3)
Cured by the Dragon (Stonefire Dragons #8)
The Dragon Warrior (Lochguard Highland Dragons #4)
Aiding the Dragon (Stonefire Dragons #9)
Finding the Dragon (Stonefire Dragons #10)
Craved by the Dragon (Stonefire Dragons #11)
The Dragon Family (Lochguard Highland Dragons #5)
Winning Skyhunter (Stonefire Dragons Universe #1)
The Dragon's Discovery (Lochguard Highland Dragons #6)

Transforming Snowridge (Stonefire Dragons Universe #2)

The Dragon's Pursuit (Lochguard Highland Dragons #7)

Persuading the Dragon (Stonefire Dragons #12)

Treasured by the Dragon (Stonefire Dragons #13)

The Dragon Collective (Lochguard Highland Dragons #8)

The Dragon's Bidder (Tahoe Dragon Mates #3)

The Dragon's Chance (Lochguard Highland Dragons #9)

Summer at Lochguard (Dragon Clan Gatherings #1)

Trusting the Dragon (Stonefire Dragons #14)

The Dragon's Memory (Lochguard Highland Dragons #10)

Finding Dragon's Court (Stonefire Dragon's Universe #3)

Taught by the Dragon (Stonefire Dragons #15)

Winter at Stonefire (Dragon Clan Gatherings #2)

Masked Dragon of Snowridge (Stonefire Dragons Universe #4)

Charming the Dragon (Stonefire Dragons #16)

The Dragon Recruit (Lochguard Highland Dragons #11)

Trahern & Grace's story (Stonefire Dragons #17, Coming Soon)

Short stories that lead up to *Persuading the Dragon* / *Treasured by the Dragon*:

Meeting the Humans (Stonefire Dragons Shorts #1)

The Dragon Camp (Stonefire Dragons Shorts #2)
The Dragon Play (Stonefire Dragons Shorts #3)
Dragon's First Christmas (Stonefire Dragons Shorts #4)

Semi-related dragon stories set in the USA, beginning sometime around *The Dragon's Discovery / Transforming Snowridge*:

The Dragon's Choice (Tahoe Dragon Mates #1)
The Dragon's Need (Tahoe Dragon Mates #2)
The Dragon's Bidder (Tahoe Dragon Mates #3)
The Dragon's Charge (Tahoe Dragon Mates #4)
The Dragon's Weakness (Tahoe Dragon Mates #5)
The Dragon's Find (Tahoe Dragon Mates #6)
The Dragon's Surprise (Tahoe Dragon Mates #7 / Late Summer 2025)

Chapter One

Iris Mahajan placed a cup of tea in front of her mother, sat down at the table, and got straight to the point. "Right, you have your tea and biscuits. Now, tell me what's so important that I had to stop by immediately."

Her mother sipped her tea, then again, and Iris gripped her mug tighter in her hands. Of course she'd take her time, despite the fact Iris only had ten more minutes before she had to head into work.

Her inner dragon, the second personality inside her head, spoke up. *We're the same way, you know that. So why do you tell her to hurry when you know it'll only make her drag her feet?*

Before she could answer, her mother set her cup down and said, "Your father and I are trying to arrange a mating for you with Ashton Mitchell."

Iris blinked, and again. Ashton was a scientist on

1

Lochguard, one she hadn't exchanged more than greetings with before. "What the bloody hell are you talking about?"

Her mother tsked. "Language, Iris."

She bit back what she really wanted to say and used the tried and true, "Mu-um."

"Well, you haven't given us any choice in the matter. You're nearly thirty, you have no friends, let alone a boyfriend, and your father doesn't have all the time in the world to wait."

Her stomach dropped. "What are you talking about?"

Her mother searched her gaze for a few beats, and Iris nearly demanded an answer. But her mum finally said, "Your father is nearly twenty years older than me, and even dragon-shifters age."

"I don't think that's the full truth, aye?"

Her mother sniffed. "You're always so suspicious, Iris. Not everyone is out to deceive you and hurt you."

Not wanting to talk about her past yet again, she steered them back on topic. "So if Dad is healthy, apart from nearing seventy, then why are you trying to find me a mate? I don't want one. Bloody hell, I don't have time for one."

"Yes, yes, work. Always work with you. But it wasn't always that way once."

"Don't use that against me, Mum. That was a long time ago."

"If I truly thought you didn't want a mate, I would

back off." Iris opened her mouth, but her mother beat her to it. "You're lonely, Iris. You try to hide it, but I'm your mother, and I see it."

Iris tried not to shift in her seat. Few could endure the stare of Jhanvi Mahajan and keep quiet. It was why she did so well working in the clan archives—one look would quiet anyone.

Her dragon spoke up again. *She's right, though. You can hide it from everyone but me. And I wouldn't mind a mate.*

You just want someone to fuck on a regular basis.

Maybe. But I also would like for you to be happy. And you're not.

Her mother reached across the table and touched Iris's hand. "Do you know why I named you Iris?"

"Aye, of course—"

Her mother cut her off. "No, I think you forget. The flower often symbolizes hope, wisdom, trust, and valor. You were the hope of our new start here in the UK. And whilst you're very clever and have lived up to the valor part, you need to learn to trust others, Iris. Even just a little."

"I trust you and Dad."

"And that's a start. But I don't want to see my only daughter so lonely all the time. Find a friend, even. Maybe later you can find a mate."

She was about to repeat she didn't need any distractions from her job when her Protector-only mobile phone rang. The ringtone was for Cooper Maxwell,

Lochguard's second-in-command of security. She whispered, "I have to take this," and hit the Receive button. "Cooper?"

"Iris, come to the surgery right away."

She stood. "Why, what happened?"

"It's Faye."

Faye MacKenzie was one of the co-leaders of the Protectors on Lochguard. She was also pregnant with her second child. "The bairn?"

"Safe for now. But Grant wants to speak with us."

"Aye, I'm on my way."

She ended the call and looked at her mother. "I have to go, Mum. Faye's at the surgery."

"Is she okay?"

"For now." She kissed her mother's cheek. "I'll stop by later."

With that, Iris dashed out of her parents' house and ran toward the surgery. While she wasn't as close with Faye as she could be, Iris respected her. And the thought of anything happening to the female made her heart twist.

Her dragon spoke up. *Between Grant and Dr. MacFarland, she's in good hands.*

Not wanting to argue, she ran faster. Iris had just entered and skidded to a halt when Cooper waved at her from reception. She stopped next to him, and he said, "That was fast."

"Aye, well, I can't help it if you're a slow runner."

His lips twitched. "Let's not bring up my loss again." He gestured with his hand. "Follow me."

They walked down a hallway until they reached one of the patient rooms. Cooper knocked before entering.

Faye lay on a hospital bed, propped up on pillows. Her mate and other co-protector, Grant McFarland, stood next to her, holding her hand.

Faye met her gaze and smiled. "I'm fine."

Grant grunted. "You aren't."

A throat cleared from behind her, and Iris turned to see Dr. Layla McFarland—the clan's head doctor and Grant's sister-in-law. Layla entered and stood on the other side of Faye's bed. "Well, you're both right."

Grant frowned. "What do you mean?"

The doctor answered, "Faye and the bairn are fine. This time. Faye had a difficult pregnancy with your daughter, and this one looks to be no different. Which means she needs to take it easy."

Faye scowled. "Please tell me it's not bed rest again this time around."

"Trust me, I understand, aye? I had to endure that too. But whilst it hasn't reached that point yet, you need to ease back on your Protector duties until the bairn is born." Layla glanced at Iris and Cooper before saying, "I need all of you to make sure she follows my orders, aye?"

Grant nodded. "I'll make sure she takes it easy, Layla. That's why I called Cooper and Iris here."

Layla said, "Right, well, I'll come back in about ten

minutes to go over Faye's restrictions for the next six months."

Once the doctor was gone, Grant looked at Cooper and then Iris before saying, "The two of you have been asking for more responsibilities for ages, aye? Well, with Faye and Isla needing me, I'm going to have to step back a little as well. Which means you two will need to handle most of the clan matters until our bairn is born."

Iris was torn between concern for Faye and excitement at this opportunity. After all, she'd been waiting for years to be given more duties.

Cooper spoke up. "Aye, we'll do whatever you need, Grant, Faye."

"Yes, we'll do whatever you need," Iris stated.

Faye said, "Aye, well, you might not be so happy about it once we fill you in on a few things."

Grant lifted a hand and brushed some of Faye's curly hair from her face. "We can do that later, love. Right now, you need to rest."

As the pair stared at one another, their eyes full of love, a stab of jealousy rushed through Iris. At one time, she'd dreamed of having that kind of love forever.

Until reality had taught her it was foolish.

Her dragon spoke up. *We could still have it, if you only looked and opened up to people.*

Thankfully, Cooper cleared his throat to prevent her from replying to her beast and asked, "Is there anything immediate we need to know? If not, then we can leave you two to talk with the doctor and we'll chat later."

Faye's eyes shot to Iris's. "Actually, there is."

She didn't like the look in Faye's eyes. "What is it?"

"This afternoon is our monthly report meeting with you-know-who."

Her stomach dropped. No. Not *him*.

Before Iris could protest, Faye continued, "I want both of you to meet with Antony Holbrook. If there's anything you can't answer, then ring us, aye? But between the pair of you, it should be fine."

Iris wanted to make excuses and say Cooper could handle Antony. But that would be cowardly and might make Faye and Grant rethink their decision about giving her more responsibility.

Her dragon snorted. *Out of everyone to be afraid of, he's an odd choice, aye?*

You just want to ogle him again.

Why not? He's fit, and I wouldn't mind riding him.

Not wanting to get into the same argument yet again with her dragon, Iris nodded. "Aye, we'll handle it. The two of you focus on your family."

Once she and Cooper had said their goodbyes, they headed toward the main Protector building. The entire walk, her dragon flashed images of Antony's tall, lean figure, his light brown hair sprinkled with silver, and his piercing brown eyes. Ones that always seemed as if they could see straight into her soul.

By the time she reached her office, she shut the door and growled at her dragon. *Stop it.*

Why? It's been a long, long time since we've had sex.

7

He seems like the kind of male who would be up for it with no strings attached.

No. I won't risk him being my true mate.

Then don't kiss him.

I don't plan on kissing anyone.

Then Mum will push Ashton again.

There was nothing wrong with the male. Well, apart from him still grieving for his dead sister. He coped by obsessing over finding a way to save others.

She replied to her beast, *I can handle Mum. Don't worry.*

She's just as stubborn as you. Don't forget that, aye?

As if she could. *I have work to do.*

Fine. Besides, I want to be alert when Antony gets here.

Her dragon yawned and curled up into a ball inside her head. Once her beast was asleep, Iris sat at her desk and tried to focus on work.

And as she went over the new information Grant had sent her, she forgot all about Antony Holbrook and his simultaneously charming-yet-annoying self.

Chapter Two

As Antony Holbrook changed gears to slow down his car, he was careful not to wince. Three broken ribs bloody well hurt, but he'd endured worse.

Far worse.

He glanced at the woman in the passenger's seat, and she snorted. "I told you to let me drive. I bet that hurt like hell, didn't it?"

"Hush."

"Nope."

She grinned, and he rolled his eyes. Katrina Lau was one of the few people he trusted, and the only one who knew he'd been beaten to a bloody pulp during their last assignment.

It'd taken a lot of bribing to keep his superiors from finding out, but it'd been worth it. Otherwise, they might start suggesting he retire again.

And Antony wasn't ready to do that. He was far from his dotage.

He turned onto the road leading to Clan Lochguard and steeled himself for another gear change as they approached the gate.

Trina said, "There are cars with automatic transmissions. You should try one."

"It will be a cold day in hell before I do that."

Pain radiated from his side again. But after his decades-long work for a secret division of MI5, he had a better poker face than just about anyone.

After they cleared the gates and he parked in front of the dragon security building, he glanced at Trina. "This is your last chance to change your mind. Because as soon as we head inside, you'll have no choice but to go to Stonefire."

Clan Stonefire was the dragon-shifter clan in the north of England. It was also where Trina's half-sister, Nikki Gray-Hartley, helped run their clan security. And she didn't know that Trina even existed.

She raised a dark eyebrow. "I would think I've proven myself enough times by now for you to trust my decisions, Antony. And I already made this one."

"You have. But this is different, and you know. If you can't recognize..."

She finished, "A possible weakness, then everyone could get hurt or die."

"Exactly."

"I know, I know. And I plan to be upfront with Nikki, the first chance I get."

"That will still be some weeks away. We have to finish this next assignment first."

She shrugged. "If no one has made the connection after all these years, a few more weeks won't hurt."

He'd suggested she talk to the dragonwoman earlier, but Trina had wanted some time to prepare. Nikki would no doubt have questions, and some of them weren't easy to answer. Even Antony knew that.

He searched Trina's brown-eyed gaze and nodded. "Right, then you handle it as you see fit. For now, let's deliver this news before it leaks to the press."

And it would, sooner or later. If it didn't surface by tomorrow, his superior would do it himself.

Slowly, Antony rose out of the car and straightened his shirt and jacket. Part of him pitied Faye and Grant, who had no idea of the media storm coming their way.

And yet, a sense of excitement thrummed through him. Because he might see *her* again soon.

The dragonwoman he liked to ruffle, whenever he got the chance. Even though he shouldn't.

In general, Antony kept his distance from people. Well, apart from his brother, Max, and Max's mate, Lavinia.

However, staying in contact with his brother was risky, and the sensible thing to do would be to stay away. And yet, Antony hadn't been able to cut Max out of his life. It was almost as if his brother were the last link he had to being human, and if Antony gave him up, he might turn into a monster.

You're careful, don't worry. It won't be like before. Not wanting to think about the person he'd lost years ago because of his ego and recklessness, Antony pushed aside thoughts of family and the past before donning his charming persona. A younger dragon-shifter, not more than twenty or so, sat at the security reception desk. He stood as Antony and Trina stopped in front of him. "Hello, I'm Antony Holbrook. I have an appointment."

"Of course, Mr. Holbrook. Although things have changed a wee bit."

"How so?"

"Aye, well, see for yourself."

Antony hated surprises because then he couldn't plan for the eventual attack. "Tell me what's changed, young man. Otherwise, I'll turn around and drive off."

Trina was used to his ways and remained silent.

The young dragonman frowned. "No need to be so dramatic, aye? It's just that Faye and Grant are busy, so you'll be meeting with Iris and Cooper."

He made a mental note to find out what had happened to the co-head Protectors. If his protégé was as good as he knew she was, Trina would already know the answer by the end of his meeting.

As if reading his mind, the woman spoke up. "I'm supposed to inspect the Protector drills today. So, if someone could show me the way?"

The dragonman motioned someone over, and

Antony recognized the tall dragonwoman with dark skin, black hair, and brown eyes—she was Zoe Watson. They'd worked together during a recent mission involving a geocaching competition.

She nodded at him and then asked the dragonman, "What's up?"

"The female is here to watch the Protector drills." He frowned and glanced at Trina. "Sorry, what is your name?"

She smiled, and the dragonman blinked. Yes, his protégé was bringing out the charm. She answered, "Trina is fine. And you are?"

"Er, Arran."

As he gaped at Trina, Zoe snorted. "And this is why you're doing reception work, Arran. You need to learn how to resist a bonny face."

Arran glared. "I would say more, but we have guests, aye? I know how to act."

Zoe shook her head and turned toward Trina. "I'm Zoe. And I'll take you, but you do know they don't start for twenty minutes, aye?"

Trina nodded. "Yes, but my boss here is eager to talk with the Protectors in charge. He'll just get grumpy if I'm in the room. I'd rather stare at the sky than deal with that."

Antony bit back a smile and appeared to be a tad bit annoyed. "She's right—I need to share sensitive information with Iris and Cooper, and she can't hear it. So would you take her, even if it's just to stare at the sky? Us mere humans don't get to see dragons this close very often."

In truth, Trina already knew everything but had come precisely to listen to clan gossip and report back to him.

She played her part and smiled at Arran again. "Or, you could show me what you do here? I don't get to visit with dragon-shifters very often, you know. And I'm oh-so curious to learn as much as possible."

Arran cleared his throat, but Zoe rolled her eyes and gestured. "The lad will never get anything done then. Come on, follow me."

As the two women went off, Antony mentally laughed at the dejected look on Arran's face. He couldn't be more than twenty-two or so, and it showed. Antony asked, "Pray tell, what is your full name?"

"Arran MacPherson."

"Right, Mr. MacPherson. If Iris and Cooper are ready, then show me the way."

Thankfully, the dragonman pulled it together, and Antony followed him down the corridor to a familiar meeting room used for non-clan members. Ever since he'd helped Emma McAllister and Logan Lamont—or, rather, they had helped him—Antony had been visiting Lochguard at regular intervals. Mainly because the Scottish dragon clan was closest to his little problem, one his superiors wanted dealt with sooner rather than later. Especially given what had happened in recent days.

Arran knocked and twisted the knob. Inside, the

dragonman named Cooper Maxwell stared down at his phone. Next to him sat Iris Mahajan. Her dark brown eyes met his gaze, and a shock of lust rushed through him.

What would it be like to see her completely naked and at ease? Maybe even laughing?

Stop it. He wasn't a young buck any longer, and he needed to harness his legendary control. While he had some sort of strange pull toward the dragonwoman, it wasn't as if he could do anything but tease her.

He refused to risk her life.

Focusing on what he could do, he smirked and asked, "Happy to see me like always, my dear?"

"More like I'm busy, so get started already."

Cooper gave her a look—no doubt because the dragonwoman always seemed so cool with others—but Antony focused on her. "Ah, but small talk keeps us all civil." He brushed invisible lint off his sleeve before tugging at his shirt cuff. "And I'd rather not talk about the weather. But if you've heard of any unique bird sightings, then do tell."

"What the bloody hell are you talking about? You're into birds now?"

He ignored Cooper's deepening frown. "I always have been, my dear. One needs something to do when hunkered down in a forest, waiting for prey."

Cooper cleared his throat, and Antony finally forced his gaze to the dragonman and smiled. "Hello, old chap. It's been a while, hasn't it?"

He blinked. "Er, yes. But Iris is right—we have a lot to do today. So if you could sit and get started, that would be helpful."

Antony glanced from one to the other. "Is there anything I can assist with?"

Iris shook her head. "No. We have it in hand."

No doubt she did. But he still replied, "I'm always here, if you should need me."

She muttered, "I bloody well won't."

Antony chuckled as he sat down, careful not to wince at the pain in his ribs. "That may change, sooner than you think." He held out a file folder and tossed it onto the table. "The clanless dragon-shifters living in Cairngorms National Park have disappeared."

Over the years, as more clans accepted humans, some dragon-shifters had tried to keep dragon clans for dragons only. Eventually, those who resisted the changes had been banished or ran away. The majority of them had gathered together in Cairngorms.

It was something all the UK dragon clans had been watching closely. But not as closely as Antony and his superiors.

Cooper frowned. "So they've moved? To where?"

"No, they haven't moved—they've vanished. And before you ask, we've been watching that site for a long time now. If they so much as took a piss, we knew." He leaned forward. "And yet one day, the site was simply abandoned, with us none the wiser. It's as if a portal opened up and swallowed them."

Or, he had a traitor in his midst that had helped them. But one thing at a time.

Iris rolled her eyes. "This isn't some science-fiction show, Holbrook. They had to go somewhere."

"Indeed. Certain individuals are eager to find out where." He tapped the file folder. "This will all leak by tomorrow, at the latest. We want to judge the public's reaction and see if it helps answer the question of where they bloody went."

Cooper jumped in. "But won't that just send people to the dragon clans, saying we murdered our own kind, and cause chaos?"

"Perhaps. But we need to see how your enemies react to the news."

As well as other dragon-shifters, but he couldn't share that bit. Not yet.

Iris said, "That includes how the dragon hunters react, aye?"

"Yes, my dear. Especially them. But there are also people on the internet who stir the pot all the time. Some of it is to be cruel, and others genuinely want a human and dragon war. So we'll be monitoring them, too." He gestured toward the file folder. "Inside is information the media won't get, so study it and let me know if you have any questions."

He stood slowly and Iris asked, "You're just going to drop that bombshell and leave?"

Raising an eyebrow, he replied, "That file will

answer your questions, and then some. It's better for you two to study it and then ask me questions later."

"How can we when you always disappear into the ether?" Iris asked.

Antony took out a small phone and held it out. "This is your direct line of contact to me. It can't be traced, nor will it dial any number but the one in there."

She took it, careful not to brush her fingers against his. But Antony couldn't resist, and reached out his forefinger to touch her thumb as she pulled away.

Like always, electricity raced through him at her touch. Her pupils flashed between round and slitted, too.

Ah, so she wasn't as unaffected as she pretended to be.

Don't think of it. Not even once. It's too risky. Antony dropped his hand and nodded. "If anything happens, anything at all, let me know. You may also want to watch the family members here who have a relative or loved one who left back when Finn gave his ultimatum."

At one point, some of the Lochguard dragon-shifters had wanted to hurt Arabella, Finn Stewart's mate, and get rid of any humans. In the end, the Lochguard clan leader had banished anyone who wouldn't follow his leadership or accept humans.

Cooper shared a glance with Iris and finally replied, "Aye, we've been doing that already, but we'll increase our surveillance."

"On all of them?"

As if he didn't know Grant McFarland's father and uncle had left Lochguard years ago with the traitors.

Iris frowned. "Some of them would die for the clan, like Grant. So, no, we won't watch *all* of them."

He smirked. "I was just testing you two. I already know Grant and his brother, Chase, can be trusted."

Iris stood. "Then why waste our time?"

"Because sometimes you can learn a lot from a person's reaction." She opened her mouth, but Antony beat her to it. "Right, then I'm off. If I don't hear from you, I'll return in a few weeks. Our meetings will be more frequent, as a matter of national security."

Before either dragon could say a word, Antony turned and exited the room. If he'd stayed, he would've been tempted to tease Iris some more. And nothing good could come from it. Distance was the only way to navigate his life and his work.

Because he would never again cause someone else's death, like he'd done with his late fiancée.

Chapter Three

As soon as Antony was gone, Iris turned to Cooper. "Should we wait until after Faye's out of the hospital before we tell Grant about this?"

"Aye, I think so. They put us in charge, so let's study what we have first and then discuss how to broach the topic with Faye and Grant."

Iris reached for the file folder, but before she could open it, Cooper lightly slapped his hand on top of it. "What's between you and Antony Holbrook?"

Her dragon hummed. *Nothing. Yet. But I can tell he wants us.*

We're not talking about this.

Iris replied to Cooper, "Nothing. He's a pain in my arse, that's all. His brother, Max, let slip one time that since Antony is usually isolated, he likes to annoy as many people as possible when he gets the chance."

"He didn't annoy me." Cooper searched her gaze. "Holbrook fancies you. Maybe he's your true mate."

Panic surged through Iris. "No, he can't be."

"But what if he is? Don't you want to know?"

"No." She reached for the folder again and tugged it closer. "I know you want nothing more than to find yours, but some of us want to focus on our jobs and careers instead."

She wondered if Cooper would push, but he merely shrugged. "It's your life, not mine. Just promise me that if something happens, you'll tell me, aye?"

"Nothing will happen, I promise. Now, let's focus and find out what happened to the rogue dragons."

As they each took some papers from the folder, her dragon spoke up. *You can pretend with Cooper, but I know Antony's touch affected us. Maybe we should call him and see if he answers.*

Don't be ridiculous. The phone is for emergencies.

Us finally getting some sex is an emergency.

Enough. I need to concentrate. So will you be quiet or do I have to construct a mental maze?

Her beast sniffed. *Do your boring human stuff.*

As her dragon settled down for a nap inside her head, Iris focused on the documents.

She was impressed with how thorough they were. Antony hadn't been boasting when he'd said they watched the rogue dragons closely. Every movement, every dragon taking off with their color and markings noted, was here. They'd kept track of everything for years.

For a split second, Iris wondered if maybe Lochguard should've been paying closer attention. Oh, aye, they knew where the rogue dragons stayed, and thanks to Iris's contacts around Scotland, she knew when and where they flew.

And yet, when night fell or if there was a storm, her informants couldn't help her. That was a weakness she should've recognized sooner.

Her dragon's voice was sleepy as she said, *Stop trying to be responsible for all security on Lochguard. You are one of many.*

Cooper's voice prevented Iris from replying to her beast. "Here's where all their activity stopped. Take a look, Iris."

She quickly scanned the document and said, "It really was like they fell through a portal and vanished. One day, they were flying and hunting and quietly visiting villages, and the next, nothing."

"And what's strange is that everything was left in a hurry—dishes on makeshift tables, clothes drying on lines, and even a few toys stacked in the middle of a clearing."

She'd known about some of the rogue dragons having bairns over the years, but for the first time, she wondered how they were doing living outside a clan.

But she pushed that aside and focused. "Maybe

there was some kind of danger. Or, this is all part of a plan."

"Aye, well, we need more than what's in this folder. We should call Holbrook and see if he has more answers."

Iris shook her head. "No, there's a better way. Nothing beats flying to a location and investigating it ourselves."

She stood, and Cooper followed. "Hold on, Iris. I know you're a bloody good tracker and have more contacts in Scotland than anyone. However, some of the worst of dragonkind lived in those forests, and if something made them run, it can't be good, aye?"

"I know that. But this will leak by tomorrow, Cooper. If I don't go now, we'll lose our chance. And my gut says I should go."

Cooper searched her gaze, and she resisted growling or tapping her foot. He was one of the few people on Lochguard she trusted with her life. They'd served together in the British Army, and he'd stood up for her when others had tried to steal credit for her work or pressure her to quit.

He didn't doubt her abilities. No, he cared about her as a friend, no matter how much she'd tried to keep him at a distance, like everyone else.

Iris softened her voice. "Cooper, you know deep down that I need to investigate whilst we still can. I'll be careful, aye? And you can even give me a check-in time."

He raised an eyebrow. "Will you follow it?"

"I'll try this time, I promise."

Cooper grunted. "Fine. But only if you take Holbrook's phone with you, in addition to the untrace-able one for the Protectors. And more importantly, you'll promise to reach out to the human male if you need to. Holbrook has resources we can only dream of."

"Aye, I will. But time is of the essence, and I need to go now. The news hasn't broken yet, and the clock's ticking."

"Go, then. But come back as soon as you can, Iris. The last thing I need is to finally get more responsibility and then lose one of the best Protectors in the country."

"Are you trying to butter me up?"

"No, I mean it. And sometimes, I think you need to hear it. Maybe one day you'll stop trying to prove yourself. Especially since you don't need to do it here, of all places."

Her dragon spoke up. *He's right.*

Ignoring her beast, Iris replied to Cooper, "Aye, well, then I'm off. I'll be in and out as quickly as I can. In the meantime, can you double-check the list of everyone who has a relative, former friend, or loved one that left Lochguard and joined the rogue dragons? I want to make sure we didn't miss anyone, not even someone distantly related."

He tapped his temples. "I already have the list in my head and have gone over it many times. There are a few I think we should watch closely, to see how they react to the news about the dragons vanishing. I'll also debrief

Finn, plus assign extra patrols around the perimeter in case angry humans show up once the news leaks."

She studied her colleague, who was probably the closest thing she had to a friend. "Having more responsibility suits you."

"Same for you. Now, let's prove we can do this, Iris. Lochguard is going to need us more than ever."

She bobbed her head. "Aye, I'm off. We'll meet up once I get back and then talk to Grant. It won't be easy for him."

"It won't be easy for a lot of people here. And remember, Iris, asking for help isn't a weakness. We need you to come back in one piece."

Not wanting to discuss it further, Iris waved and walked down the corridor. Soon she exited to the landing area behind the Protector building and stripped her clothes. Once she'd stowed them and her mobile phones in a satchel she could carry in her dragon form—the last thing she needed was for humans to see her naked and freak out—she closed her eyes. Her nose elongated into a snout, wings sprouted from her back, and legs stretched until she stood in her purple dragon form.

Her beast flapped their wings a few times. *I wish we had time to test out some new maneuvers.*

They both enjoyed pushing themselves to the limit in the air. *Once all of this mess is sorted, I'll make time.*

For real this time?

Aye, for real. Now, let's take the least populated route to Cairngorms National Park and see what we can find.

Iris reveled in the wind brushing against their scales. She often felt more at ease in the air, where she could better watch out for threats.

Since it wasn't time to admire the hills, lochs, or valleys below, she concentrated on the cars, people, and aircraft. Since it was midday during the week, the roads and air were fairly empty. And thankfully, they soon reached the boundary of the national park. From here, things would be a bit more tricky. The rogue dragons were good at camouflage.

She used the clouds as much as possible to keep herself hidden—one benefit of living in Scotland was that there were a lot of cloudy days—and spotted the small loch the rogue dragons used for water and swimming. At least, according to both her records and Antony's. Maybe they'd changed locations, but it was worth a look.

As she slowly descended to a clearing she'd used before for surveillance, her dragon spoke up. *What's that strange smell?*

She'd been so focused on looking for enemies that Iris hadn't noticed. But now she took a deep inhalation and nearly grimaced. *I don't know. But it smells like rotting rubbish mixed with rotten eggs.*

Wanting to see if she could detect any other scents, she took a few more deep breaths. However, after the third one, her wings faltered. Even when her beast tried to correct it, they plummeted. Only through some half-arsed attempts to widen her wings did she manage to slow down a little.

Hitting the ground, they turned the landing into a roll. They tumbled through the small trees, hitting branches and bushes as they went, until they crashed into a stone cottage. The bones in one of her wings cracked, pain shot through her body, and she barely held back a cry.

Iris said to her dragon, *We have to keep going.*

It hurts. More than ever before.

I know, dragon. And we'll fix it as soon as we can. But the gas, or whatever it is, wasn't by accident. Someone will come looking.

There's a smaller loch on the other side of the hill. Swimming will be easier than hobbling.

Agreeing with her beast, Iris stood up. Since she could still smell the awful substance, she held her breath as much as possible while they struggled up the small hill. Her human form would be easier to maneuver, but she wouldn't risk it. Her injuries would heal faster in her dragon form, and Iris needed every advantage she could get.

Foot by agonizing foot, Iris crawled to the top of the small hill. But once she reached the top, a wave of dizziness washed over her and she struggled to keep her eyes open.

Her dragon spoke up. *Roll down the hill. It'll bloody hurt, but it's our best option.*

Even with water to break our fall, I don't want to drown if we pass out.

The cold water should help keep us awake long enough to reach the far shore.

She eyed it in the distance. Like most lochs in Scotland, it was long and narrow, and she wasn't sure she could swim that far.

But as another blast of the foul scent hit her nose, making her dizzier, Iris knew they had to get away or they'd be sitting ducks.

And would probably end up disappearing like the rogue dragons.

Bracing herself for the oncoming pain, her dragon rolled them down the hill. She nearly roared in agony every time something bumped against her damaged wing. By the time they hit the water, Iris and her beast struggled to remain conscious.

But the blast of arctic water jolted them, and with their forelimbs and hind legs, they swam. By the time they reached the far shore, dots swam before her eyes. Using the last of their strength, they got out of the loch and crawled to a small copse of trees. It wasn't much to hide them, but it was the best they could do.

Because within seconds of reaching it, the world went black.

Chapter Four

E verything hurt, but her wing worst of all. That was the first thought that went through Iris's mind as she started to regain consciousness.

Opening her eyes was hard, but eventually she lifted her eyelids. She was still in her dragon form, but the giant room, mostly empty except for the big bed she lay on, was foreign.

Slowly, she looked around at three bare walls and one made of clear glass, and she struggled to her feet.

Where are we?

Her beast replied, *I don't know. But if someone doesn't stop the constant beeping of that bloody machine, I'm going to hit it across the room with my tail.*

Iris had seen something like it before, whenever a dragon was hurt back on Lochguard. However, this most definitely wasn't Lochguard. At home, injured dragons recovered in big tents that were constructed around them. There certainly wasn't a room like this one.

As she wondered if she'd been captured by the dragon hunters, a human male walked in front of the glass.

And not just any human, but Antony Holbrook.

For a split second, pain raced through her, but of the emotional variety—hurt, anger, confusion, and even failure. She'd almost trusted him, her gut had said to trust him, and yet he'd brought her to this strange place.

He might have even developed the gas that had made her crash and fall unconscious.

After pressing something to the side of the window, his voice echoed in the room. "Stop looking at me as if I kicked your puppy, Iris. My people were watching the site and saw you crash. We brought you here to recover."

She wanted to believe him, wanted to demand more information, and yet she couldn't shift back to a human until she'd healed more.

As if reading her thoughts, Antony spoke again. "If you won't believe me, maybe you'll believe her."

A dragonwoman with brown hair, pale skin, and a single scar on her cheek walked in front of the glass. She was a doctor from Clan Skyhunter who'd come several times to visit Aimee King—a Skyhunter dragonwoman staying on Lochguard. But even so, Iris didn't know Dr. Scarlett Turner very well.

The dragonwoman glanced at Antony and then looked back at Iris. She held up something like a walkie-talkie to her face and her southern English accent filled the room. "Seeing as you interviewed me on my first visit to Lochguard, I hope you remember me. But I'm Dr. Scarlett Turner, from Skyhunter."

Iris grunted, hoping the dragonwoman understood her question: *Where am I?*

Scarlett replied, "You're in quarantine, near London. And since I've been helping Mr. Holbrook with other dragon medical matters, he called in a favor to get me to help you."

As Scarlett's pupils flashed, Iris's dragon spoke up. *I believe her.*

So easily? You know she was imprisoned and tortured by Skyhunter's former leader. No doubt she's a master at hiding her emotions.

Maybe. But Aimee trusts her. And that speaks volumes.

While the former Skyhunter leader had imprisoned anyone who'd challenged his orders, he'd hurt some of his clan members more than others. Aimee had been young, so very young, when she'd been imprisoned and tortured. And for months after arriving on Lochguard, she'd stayed inside her cottage and never talked.

With time, between Arabella's help—she'd suffered her own torture as a teen under the dragon hunters—and a burgeoning friendship with Connor MacAllister, Aimee had slowly come out of her shell.

So for Aimee to trust Scarlett meant Iris wouldn't

completely disregard the dragonwoman. At least, not yet.

The doctor spoke again. "And one more thing before I go. I've been developing a prototype that will translate your thoughts whilst in your dragon form into a voice. It's had some glitches, but I think I've fixed most of them. If you're interested, I'll get it ready. So either nod or shake your head."

Iris blinked. One of the biggest weaknesses of a dragon-shifter being in their dragon forms was the inability to speak.

Her beast said, *Then we should try it. It could help us in our fight against the dragon hunters. Just imagine how much time it'd save us, too, from always having to shift to give commands or rely on wing signals.*

She eyed the Skyhunter doctor. But despite her best stare down, the other female never looked away or blinked.

Iris finally nodded, and the doctor spoke up again. "Brilliant. The next time I suit up and check your injuries, we can attach it to your temples. Give me a few hours to make some last-minute adjustments with my team, and I'll be back."

With that, she walked out of Iris's sight.

Antony still stood in front of the glass, and his lips twitched as he said, "Dr. Turner isn't my biggest fan, I'm afraid. She thinks I could've single-handedly saved her and the others on Skyhunter much sooner. However, it wasn't that simple."

Why not? She wanted to ask.

Antony continued talking, as if she'd spoken. "You'll find out that answer, and more, once you heal, my dear. For now, I just wanted to see that you were indeed awake. Because for a while there, we weren't sure if you'd survive or not. Another thirty seconds of that gas, and you wouldn't be here." He leaned closer to the glass. "What the bloody hell were you thinking, Iris? Going straight to the site without a word or checking in with me. You could've died."

She growled. So much for Antony trusting and believing her. He was just another male who thought a female couldn't handle herself in dangerous situations.

Her dragon sighed. *I don't think that's it.*

Then what?

I think he was worried about us. He might even care a wee bit.

She mentally snorted. *Stop trying to romanticize things, dragon.*

Before her beast could reply, Antony's voice filled the room again. "As much as some men love to have one-sided conversations, I'm not one of them. I'll be back to see you after Dr. Turner tests the prototype. Because otherwise, it could be days before you can shift back into your human form. And I'd very much like to discuss a few things with you."

She studied the human. But his face had the usual cocky-and-nearly-amused expression he almost always had with her. The only time she'd seen him drop it was with his brother, Max.

Or the very brief flash of anger when he'd mentioned her dying.

Her dragon spoke up. *I think he likes us.*

Before she could reply to her beast, Antony turned and walked out of her sight. Iris wanted to roar and scream. He and Scarlett had told her almost nothing. And now she'd have to sit on her arse or sleep so her body could heal.

And she bloody well hated being idle for so long.

Her dragon spoke up. *Sleep. We need to heal, and whilst you might fight it, I know how exhausted we are.*

Fine. But let's hope that prototype works, because I'll go mad if I can't get some answers soon.

After turning a few circles on the large bed, she finally curled into a ball and closed her eyes. And as she drifted off, some music played over the speakers. Although how the people running the facility knew one of her favorite bands, she had no idea.

Antony tried to distract himself with paperwork.

But every time he tried to write something, his mind drifted back to seeing Iris in her dragon form, unconscious, her wing bone poking out of her skin. His stomach had dropped, and flashbacks to Lisa's death had nearly overwhelmed him.

Which was ridiculous, since he barely knew Iris Mahajan. Yes, he liked to tease her. And she was fucking clever, beautiful, and a bloody good tracker.

And yet, for a split second, when he'd thought she was dead, his heart had twisted.

You're getting too close, Holbrook. You need to put distance between you, more than before, or Iris will pay the price.

At least he'd called in some favors to get her to this facility. Once she healed and returned to Scotland, he'd find a way to avoid her as much as possible.

He'd just attempted to answer the same question for the eighth time when a member of his team, Joseph Doyle, walked through his office door.

The tall dragonman with pale skin, blond hair, and green eyes never smiled unless he was on a job. But he was one of Antony's best team members, someone who could get information from just about anyone. And all without harsh tactics.

How, he'd never know. Maybe he just stared them down.

Antony abandoned his paperwork and asked, "What do you want, Joseph?"

The man's Northern Irish accent filled the room. "They've finished analyzing that substance you found. It's a diluted neurotoxin, one that only affects dragon-shifters and not humans."

"Fuck. It's like we thought, then. Someone has started using bioweapons."

Joseph sat in the chair in front of Antony's desk. "The scientists are still trying to find any kind of signature to hint at who made it. But they won't be able to do it without help. I want to investigate, but I need your okay to do it alone."

"No. You have a partner, and per protocol, you go together."

The other man crossed his arms over his chest. "He's human and only slows me down."

Antony raised an eyebrow. "As am I. But who was it that kicked your arse when you tried to attack me, back when you were a teenager and full of far too much anger?"

Joseph grunted. "That was different. You were younger, and I was weaker."

"Ah, so I'm an old pensioner now," he drawled. "Good to know."

"Antony," he growled.

"Fine, fine. I'll get back to the point—Gavin Edwards is one of the best spies in the United Kingdom. He can get in and out of places we can only imagine. Besides, if you're investigating a drug that can kill dragon-shifters, then it might be a good idea to have a human around to save you, if you're exposed."

The dragonman grunted again, and Antony resisted rolling his eyes. Sometimes, managing a human-dragon team of highly skilled but socially awkward or stunted individuals was challenging. Of course, living on the edge of society would change anyone.

As he well knew.

Antony leaned back in his chair and steepled his fingers in front of him. "Take Gavin with you for this investigation, and I'll reconsider approving your transfer to Northern Ireland."

"Really? You'd let me leave?"

"I don't want to lose you, and I think you'll find I'm easier to work with than my Northern Irish counterpart. But yes, I will put in the transfer myself, once we've finished the case of the missing dragon-shifters. But that means working with your partner and not against him."

Antony didn't know all the details about why Joseph wanted to return to Northern Ireland, although he suspected he'd met his true mate on an assignment over there over a year ago. While the dragonman hadn't said anything specific, Antony had his sources.

Joseph nodded. "Fine, I'll do as you ask. But you'd better follow through, Antony. Or I can bloody well drag my feet in the future, if you renege."

"Right, understood. Now, go find Gavin and let me know when you're heading out."

The dragonman stood. "You'll hear from me as soon as I learn anything."

With that, Joseph strode out of Antony's office. He was just about to try doing some work again when Dr. Turner sent him a text message. Apparently, she was ready to try out the prototype with Iris.

As he made his way to the quarantine area, he imagined Iris's first words. She'd probably scold him, and for some reason, that made him smile.

Chapter Five

C ooper Maxwell was having a hell of a week.

While it'd started out fantastic, being given more responsibility by Faye and Grant, it'd only become more complicated from there.

First, his meeting with Antony Holbrook and his bombshell about the missing exiled dragon-shifters.

Then Iris went to investigate their disappearances and didn't return. Just as he'd organized a search party, Antony Holbrook had sent a message, saying Iris was with him, immediately confirmed by one of Lochguard's liaisons at the Department of Dragon Affairs, or DDA.

And now, as he stared at one of his fellow Protectors, Zoe Watson, he tried to take in what she'd just told him. "You found a human female unconscious just outside the clan's boundary?"

She nodded. "Not only that, but she was beaten up pretty badly. Dr. McFarland is doing what she can for her, but the human female has no ID, no mobile phone, nothing to tell us who she is until she wakes up."

Judging by Zoe's voice, it was more a case of *if* she woke up.

He ran a hand through his hair. "Aye, well, keep a close eye on her. As soon as the female wakes up, see if you can find out her name and if she has any family to contact. In the meantime, I'll have to reach out to the North Highland human police and ask about missing persons."

"Will they even share information with you?"

The human male in charge of the nearest station detested dragon-shifters. He kept waiting for someone from Lochguard to slip up so he could charge them.

His dragon spoke up. *I still think he'll mess up first. Then we can report him and maybe even get rid of him.*

Aye, maybe. But we have more important things to worry about. If someone got close enough to Lochguard to dump a person undetected, then we have a blind spot. And we need to find it. Fast.

He replied to Zoe, "That human will make it as difficult as possible, but I have to try, aye? If worse comes to worst, then I can contact the main Scottish police headquarters."

"I don't envy you, Cooper."

He snorted and stood. "I don't blame you. Thanks for the info, Zoe. Now, go watch over the female and let me know when she wakes up."

After following Zoe out of the room, he turned the

opposite way down the corridor and headed for one of his best friends and most trusted Protectors, Brodie MacNeil.

He found Brodie's ginger head bent over a desk with papers strewn about. The dragonman didn't even lift his face as Cooper approached. The male said, "I'm already trying to figure out *how* someone left that female here without us noticing." He clenched some papers, crumpling them. "Because if it was one of the fucking dragon hunters, it could be a warning that one of us is next."

Cooper studied his friend and his flashing dragon eyes. Brodie was usually quiet and reserved. However, Brodie's father had killed his mother before killing himself, and he took protecting females seriously, more so than anyone else.

His dragon spoke up. *Can you blame him? We have a fairly normal family, like most of Lochguard. He is one of the few clan members with a dark past.*

Aye, I know. But it also means he might push himself too far, driven by emotion instead of reason. We need to watch him, which means adding something else to my ever-growing list of duties.

You wanted the chance to be in charge of the Protectors. Personally, it's a lot of stress. I miss flying.

We'll fly as soon as I can manage it, dragon. I promise.

As his beast settled down inside his mind, Cooper clapped his friend on the shoulder. "What have you found so far, Brodie?"

He pointed to a map of the surrounding area. "She was discovered inside one of the old, abandoned cottages, here. It's one of the few with higher walls, so no one could see her from the road."

After the Highland Clearances in the 18th and 19th centuries, when many of the humans had been kicked off their land by wealthy landowners, the stone cottages had slowly rotted over time. These days, tourists came to look at them as part of a historical drive through the Highlands.

The largest group of stone ruins were just outside the clan's boundaries, which was close enough to keep most humans from trying to dump a person there.

"And the security cameras? Did they catch anything?" Cooper asked.

Brodie shook his head. "It was dark, with no moon. And since we're remote and there aren't any streetlights, nothing shows on the CCTV footage we do have."

"So someone probably came to scout the area before-hand and timed it to the new moon. Meaning, this was planned."

"Aye."

"See if we can reposition the cameras, and ask Emma or Ian MacAllister about equipment or programs that can help improve our surveillance. I don't know if whoever dumped her will return, but I want to be prepared."

Brodie glanced at him. "Iris is okay?"

Brodie, Iris, and Cooper had become a close-knit unit years ago, back in their British Army days. "Aye, as well as I can determine. Holbrook is not sharing much, but both the DDA and the Skyhunter clan leaders have confirmed she's safe. I just wish I could speak with her myself, though."

"If you need anything, just ask me, aye? Even if you're my boss now, I'm still and always will be your friend."

"Thanks, Brodie. For now, just focus on improving surveillance and discovering what happened to the human female. I should be able to handle the rest."

After Brodie asked his approval for a few more things, Cooper headed back to his office. Sitting at his desk, he eyed the mountain of paperwork needing his attention. Rubbing his face, he sighed and said to his dragon, *As much work as it is for us, I'm glad Faye doesn't have to worry about all of this right now.*

Aye, she had a difficult time with her bairns last time, and lost one. We need to look out for her.

Of course. Now, let's finish the DDA paperwork before our next meeting.

And so Cooper went to work, hoping the next day would be a wee bit easier. But given his luck, thousands of dragon hunters would show up at the clan's front gates.

His dragon sighed. *Stop it. You should worry about the humans who aren't dragon hunters showing up first.*

Thanks. That's helpful, he drawled to his beast.

Aye, well, I'm just being a realist. Better to be prepared than not.

And with that, his dragon curled up into a ball and fell asleep, leaving Cooper to wonder what else could go wrong and how he was going to tell Faye and Grant about everything without upsetting them.

Chapter Six

Excitement hummed through Dr. Scarlett Turner at the thought of testing her latest prototype, and she itched to run down the corridor. However, the last time she'd done that, someone had scolded her.

Her dragon spoke up. *Who cares? They weren't confined to an underground cell for years like we were.*

Scarlett tried not to think about the past and how her former clan leader had locked her up. The loneliness, the pain, the cold. It'd always been so cold.

And all because she'd refused to use her clan members as medical test subjects.

Those years were ones she'd rather forget, and yet no matter how much she tried, the scar running down her cheek was a constant reminder. Just seeing it in a mirror brought back memories, ones that sometimes gave her nightmares.

Scarlett pushed aside the past and replied to her beast, *After all the hoops we had to jump through to join this project, I won't risk it to save a few minutes. Besides, we're free now. That's all that matters.*

You always do that. Always push things aside. But one day, it'll break you.

I thought you were supposed to be on my side?

I am on your side. But whilst I was forced silent for a while and don't have those memories, you do. I see them sometimes, in your dreams. And you need to face the past and heal, or...

Or what? We won't find a mate? I might've wanted that once, but no more. The last time I trusted my heart to a male, he betrayed me and turned me over to him. I trust no one but my twin brother and maybe Honoria and Asher.

Honoria and Asher were the co-leaders of Clan Skyhunter. Asher had gone through a lot worse under the old leader, and Honoria had been sent away before the terror had begun. However, after taking over the clan, they'd both done their bloody best to heal everyone and improve things.

They'd even found a way for Scarlett to finish up her doctor studies, which had been nearly finished before she'd become a prisoner.

But she was still wary of some of her clan and wished like hell she wasn't.

Her dragon sighed. *Fine. I'll drop it. For now.*

However, if you're going to play with that thing, then I'm taking a nap.

Sweet dreams, dragon. Because we're here.

Scarlett stopped in front of a keypad and tapped in the code. The door opened, and she rushed the last few feet until she could see through the observation glass.

On the other side, the purple dragon form of Iris Mahajan was curled into a ball, sleeping. The sight reminded Scarlett of doing the same in her human form, wearing rags and trying to keep warm in the winter.

No. Within seconds, she forced the memory away. Iris was warm and fed and would be let out as soon as they confirmed she didn't have anything contagious or something that could be passed on.

Since it would be a few days yet before she'd know that, Scarlett headed toward the small room off to the side, where she could put on her protective gear.

It took far longer than she liked, every second dragging. She was impatient to test the latest tweaks to her dragon voice transmitter. The last test she'd been close, so very close, to fixing all the glitches. Until it'd shorted out and slightly shocked her colleague.

Crossing her fingers, she wished for things to go well. It wasn't exactly scientific, but Scarlett would take any help she could get.

After typing the code into the new keypad, she entered the large room. A second later, Iris opened her eyes, her giant slitted pupils staring at her. Slowly, the other dragonwoman lifted her head and Scarlett held up her proto-type. "Like promised, I brought it. Although I need to draw some blood and do a general examination first."

Iris bobbed her head, and Scarlett inwardly sighed with relief. Some dragon-shifters could be stubborn and irritable and grumpy when it came to doctors. Some-thing about being sick or injured and not liking to appear weak.

Thankfully, last New Year's, Scarlett had met Dr. Sid Jackson in person for the first time, and she'd learned so much from the Stonefire doctor. Some of Sid's advice came back to her: *When it comes to stubborn patients, always act as if you're the king and they must obey your every order. Obviously, they can refuse. But a dominant tone, especially coming from a female, is extremely effective.*

So, even though Iris seemed cooperative, she kept up her usual dominant doctor tone. "Right, let's get started. Lower your head and let me check your eyes, nostrils, and mouth."

After examining everything, she stated, "You're doing better. However, your eyes are still a little unfo-cused, and your nostrils are slightly swollen from the gas. But after a few more days, with enough rest, you might even be able to go home."

Antony Holbrook's voice came from speakers inside the room. "That will be up to me, Dr. Turner."

Ah, yes. The human male who liked to play with people's lives.

Her dragon's sleepy voice filled her head. *Without his help, you wouldn't be able to do your experiments. Stop blaming him for not saving Skyhunter.*

Not wanting to have the same argument again, she turned and replied to Antony, "You may try to keep her prisoner, but I won't stick around. You know there's a female on Skyhunter expecting a baby in the next two weeks. I won't abandon her."

Antony stood on the other side of the glass and shrugged. "You can go home once Iris is well. However, I have things to discuss with her in private, once she can shift into her human form again." He motioned toward the prototype she'd laid down on the side of the room. "Even if that works, I'd rather wait until Iris can't merely sit on me to quiet me down."

Iris snorted, and Scarlett glanced back at the purple dragon. "I can get him in here and you can sit on him now."

Antony sighed. "Yes, yes, pick on the human. Now, are you going to try this gadget of yours or not? Because I have things to do, Dr. Turner, no matter what you may think."

Still facing Iris, Scarlett rolled her eyes. "Fine. Give me a minute here. Now, Iris, lean your head down to my level. Yes, just like that. Right, let's get this attached."

Scarlett slowly wrapped the long strips around the dragon's head, using her ears and horns to help keep the equipment in place. Then she checked each of the diodes to make sure they lay flat against Iris's scales.

With everything secure, she flipped the little switch to turn on the speakers and stepped back. "Right, now how this works is you merely think whatever it is you or your dragon want to say and it should project it through the small speakers on your head. It may take a few tries, until the device attunes to your brain activity. After it learns your processes, it should, in theory, freely let you talk."

And so Scarlett watched Iris intently, waiting to see if her device would finally give dragon-shifters in their dragon forms the ability to talk without getting shocked.

Once the doctor finished her explanation, Iris said inside her mind, *Is this working?*

But the speakers on her head screeched and emitted, "orking?"

Close, but not quite right. So she thought it again, and after a few seconds, the speakers said in an AI-English accent, "Is this working?"

Her dragon perked up at the words just as Dr. Turner clapped her hands and said, "Keep going, Iris. Try something else. Anything. I need to see if it can handle more complex thoughts."

"Why...hell...English..."

Iris focused and tried again. "Why the bloody hell is it in an English accent?"

Dr. Turner shrugged. "That's what I have, and it's easier to project than a Scottish one."

Iris replied, "I sound bloody stupid."

Antony's voice filled the room. "Now, how about you tell me why you went off to investigate that site by yourself?"

The other dragonwoman turned toward Antony. "How about you wait until I make sure it won't short out and possibly hurt her?"

He crossed his arms over his chest, and Iris nearly snorted. It was the closest thing to irritated she'd seen from the human, and she couldn't resist saying, "Maybe I just won't talk to you, anyway."

Antony narrowed his eyes. "That would be unwise, my dear."

"Why?"

From the corner of her eye, she noticed Dr. Turner glancing between them. However, Antony's reply garnered her attention again. "Because I ultimately decide when you can leave this place."

"Are you really trying to pull a power play over me?"

"Trust me, I have connections you can only dream of, my dear. Ones I could've used to protect you if you'd just bloody rung me."

"There wasn't time. Besides, I'm not your lackey."

"Ah, but you're wrong there, Iris. Because from the second you went to investigate that site, you became my problem. And once you can shift again, we're going to discuss it."

Without another word, Antony walked out of her sight. Iris growled, hating how she couldn't follow him.

Scarlett's voice garnered her attention. "He's never shown that much emotion with anyone else, at least in my experience. But it seems you know how to get under his skin."

Iris's dragon spoke this time. "And I wouldn't mind being under him, skin-to-skin."

Silence. Scarlett just stared at her, blinking, as Iris wondered if the prototype meant she could never have a private conversation with her dragon while wearing it.

So she decided to ask. Scarlett shook her head a few times and replied, "I don't know. I was so focused on getting the thing to work that I didn't consider how *all* thoughts would be projected, both human and dragon. And that can be a bloody nuisance, with our dragon halves."

As Scarlett's pupils flashed to slits and back, Iris decided she was done voicing thoughts. "Take this off me, please. I'm tired."

As expected, the doctor moved closer and studied her. "I will, but just one last question: was there any pain or discomfort from the device on your head? And please be honest."

"No. No pain."

The doctor nodded. "Brilliant. That went better than the last time." Iris narrowed her eyes in question, and Scarlett cleared her throat before adding, "It may have shocked my last test subject. But I fixed it! Hopefully for good. Now, lower your head again, and I'll remove it."

Iris quickly asked, "When can I leave this place? Is Antony really going to keep me here?"

"In all honesty, I don't know. But he could keep you here forever, if he wanted to. I've worked with him and his team for months now, and Holbrook seems to have a lot of sway with both the human government and the DDA specifically."

"Tell me what you can."

"There's not much more I can share, without repercussions. But there is a little..."

As Scarlett removed her thought-translation device, Iris listened to the dragonwoman's information.

It wasn't much, but by the end, Iris had a slightly better idea of how things were run. Mainly, Antony was in charge of an elite team of humans and dragon-shifters. They did missions, but Scarlett didn't know the specifics. She mainly patched people up and focused on her prototypes.

Once the female finished taking off the device, Scarlett added, "I'll check in on you in a little while, after they feed you. I'll bring the interpreter device, but you don't have to use it if you don't want to. Especially if Antony is here, since your dragon might voice her lusty thoughts. Although I have to admit, his face would be priceless if she did."

Iris grunted, and Scarlett laughed. "Hey, whoever you fancy, that's your business. But I need to go. I'll see you later."

With that, the doctor left, and Iris finally spoke to

her dragon. *You would say your randy words again out loud, with him here, wouldn't you?*

Of course. Because you'd rather die than tell him you want him naked and inside us.

Being attracted to someone doesn't mean I'm going to strip and instantly ask them to fuck me.

Why not? It would make things easier.

Except humans have those pesky decency laws...

I somehow doubt Antony would report us. He wants us too.

How do you know that?

I pay attention.

That's all you're going to say?

Yes. Now, I'm tired. That took a lot of work. Let's nap.

Her beast didn't wait for a reply but instead curled up and went to sleep. And since Iris's mind hummed, she stared at the wall, wondering when she could leave and get as far away from Antony Holbrook as possible. Her dragon's interest hadn't waned with time, and that worried her.

Because if, and that was a big if, she kissed him and he turned out to be her true mate, it would ruin everything she'd ever worked for.

Chapter Seven

F ive days later, Antony sat in front of Rosalind Abbott, the Director of the Department of Dragon Affairs, and waited for her to speak. He'd been bloody summoned right before Dr. Turner's examination to determine if Iris could shift back to her human form.

But while he could technically reschedule the meeting with the DDA Director, Antony knew it might cost him a few favors. Ones he'd rather keep for later.

So he currently sat, ankle propped over his knee, and tried his best to look bored.

Rosalind finally spoke. "We need to discuss the rogue dragon problem."

"Ah, yes. So they finally showed you the report?"

"I'm going to ignore your insolence for now, only because we have more important matters to discuss.

After all, a human family discovering a mass grave of dead dragons is a ticking time bomb."

Antony had only learned of the discovery a few hours before. Even now, he had most of his team going to find out what they could. Discreetly, of course. "Keeping the humans quiet is your problem, not mine."

"Which would've been easier if the teenager hadn't live-streamed it to the world."

"I will never understand teenagers and their need to share everything. But regardless of the blip, make it seem staged. Or created with AI."

"I know how to do my job, Antony."

"Then why am I here?"

She leaned forward. "Because your team is going to work with my department on this."

He buffed his nails. "My team doesn't exist, Rosalind. Therefore, we can't work with anyone."

"The Prime Minister, as well as the heads of MI5 and MI6, all said you will this time."

Antony frowned. "What?"

"You heard me. If we can't contain this, or if more mass dragon graves are found, then the humans will panic. Probably beyond our borders, given how fast information travels these days. And as much as it pains me to say it, your team is one of the best. We need you. Please."

The DDA Director almost sounded desperate, which was new. So he dropped his act and said, "We are already working on it, which my superiors know.

Meaning there must be another reason why they ordered us to work with you."

She nodded. "Yes. For this assignment, your team is getting some new blood—some dragon-shifters and a human woman."

"Wait, no. I pick my own team members. I always have and I always will. I won't have some unvetted, bumbling idiot ruining everything."

A secret door slid open, and several familiar dragon-shifters strode in: Kai Sutherland from Stonefire, Robin Driscoll from Skyhunter, Wren Jones from Snowridge, Kaine Ferris from Northcastle, and Killian O'Shea from Glenlough.

They were all head Protectors, in charge of security for the various dragon clans.

Kai drawled, "The bumbling idiots have arrived, human."

He snorted. "And so you have."

There were a few growls, but Antony merely stood. At his full height, he was only a few inches shorter than most of the dragonmen. He looked at each in turn as he said lightly, "I may be human, but I know every single way to incapacitate a dragon-shifter. Remember that."

As Kaine opened his mouth, Rosalind stood and spoke first. "Now, now, lads, I know the lot of you are used to being in charge. But for now, you're going to work together. Antony is technically in charge, but only just. And I would think the security of your clans and countries should be more important than a figurative cock measuring contest."

The corner of Antony's mouth kicked up. "Did you just say cock, Rosalind?"

The DDA Director raised her dark eyebrows. "A woman doesn't get to where I am without hearing far worse." She looked at each person in turn. "Lochguard elected to send Iris Mahajan as their representative, given the situation on Lochguard, and she'll join you soon. For now, let's review what we know and how far you can go past the usual laws and boundaries to clean up this little problem."

As Rosalind went over things Antony already knew, he covertly studied the dragon-shifters. Throwing a tantrum would get him nowhere, but he didn't fully trust all of them. Yes, some more than others. But it would be far better to have someone from his usual crew paired up with each of them. His people would grumble, but teams would be the fastest and safest way to proceed.

And he knew exactly who would be his partner, too.

Back at the secret facility, Iris waited for Scarlett's answer. Would she finally be able to shift back to her human form?

The doctor stood inside the room, without any protective equipment, checking something on her tablet.

She wanted to scream for the female to hurry up, but knew she was just doing her job.

Besides, over the last five days, Iris had grown to like the doctor's sense of humor and honesty. Iris didn't have any female friends, really, but she kind of wanted to be Scarlett's.

Her dragon spoke up. *The lack of friends is your fault. Kiyana has invited us loads of times to have coffee or a meal, and you always brush her off.*

She always asked when I was busy. Besides, I think she only does that because Mum asked her to.

Kiyana Boyd spent a lot of time in the clan archives, researching one thing or another. And Iris's mother ran the archives.

Her dragon sighed. *I don't even know why I try.*

Scarlett's voice prevented her from replying to her beast. "Everything points to you being healthy enough to shift. However, that being said, I will need to examine and run some tests on your human form. I brought some clothes so you can spare any passing humans the embarrassment. And don't worry, Holbrook isn't here, so he won't come peek while you change." Heading toward the door, Scarlett added, "The clothes are in the room next door. I'll be back shortly to finish my examination. Fingers crossed, you'll be cleared and can join the others."

She tilted her head in question, and Scarlett shook hers. "I shouldn't have said that. Usually I'm better at keeping secrets, but I've been chattering for days to you since you can't answer without the prototype. Holbrook will fill you in once I clear you."

With that, the doctor strode out of the room, and Iris's dragon spoke up. *Let's shift so you can get answers. This stewing for days is tiring.*

I wasn't stewing.

Aye, you were since you mostly refused the thought-translator.

Only because you kept embarrassing me, dragon.

It's fun. But I want to nap, so let's shift and you can be in charge for a while.

Iris closed her eyes and imagined her wings shrinking into her back, her snout morphing back into her nose, and her limbs shortening. Within seconds, she stood in her human form and shouted, "Finally!"

Her dragon snorted. *Considering how you're usually not a big talker, it's funny how much you want to do it now.*

I talk when necessary, and there were a lot of bloody questions I need the answers to.

Iris hurried over to the small door off to the side, pressed the button, and it slid open. Once she put on the under things, jeans, shirt, and shoes Scarlett had left her, Iris stretched one way and then the other. *As much as I love you, it's nice to have a larger range of motion again.*

Remember that the next time you want to fly anywhere.

Of course you're better in the air. But on the ground, our human form is faster and more agile.

A beep sounded before Scarlett entered the room, carrying a medical bag. "Right, let's see if you're well and truly healed." Once the doctor finished her examination, she bobbed her head. "Whilst I won't get the final bloodwork for your human form for a few hours, I think you're fine. Although I need you to be brutally honest about how you feel over the next week. Any pain, dizziness, or anything that feels off, tell me, okay? Especially with what you'll be doing." She leaned over and whispered, "And keep an eye on Holbrook as well. He finally took a shot of dragon's blood for his broken ribs, but that male is bloody stubborn and could lose a limb and say he was fine."

"Aye, well, if I were sticking around, I would let you know. However, I need to go back to Lochguard."

Scarlett shook her head. "I'm afraid not. Come with me. You have a meeting with Holbrook."

"Good. Then I can tell him I'm going home in person."

The doctor glanced at her, but said nothing. Iris followed her out of the room, down the corridor, and out into a longer one.

Nondescript doors lined the walls, solid without windows and all painted white. There weren't any labels or identifying information. "What are all these rooms for?"

"I can't tell you anything yet. I wish I could, but I can't. I'm sure you understand."

Iris grunted. "So many bloody secrets."

"Yes, but they help protect our kind. Which is why, despite thinking Holbrook could've helped Skyhunter sooner, I work with him to better protect my clan now."

"You sound more like a Protector than a doctor, aye?"

Scarlett glanced at her. "Given what was done to me and the others under Marcus King, more of the doctors should've acted like Protectors."

Iris studied the dragonwoman. She'd heard a lot of rumors about Skyhunter and its former leader, but hadn't ever really asked for the truth. As she debated doing so, Scarlett stopped in front of a door and waited for it to scan her eye. The door opened, and she gestured inside. "He's in there."

"Before I head in, I just wanted to thank you for helping me."

"No worries. But in reality, you helped me just as much with my prototype."

"And you'll let me know when we can try them out on Lochguard?"

Scarlett smiled. "I hope soon. But I'll push to make your clan the test one."

"Not your own?"

"Well, let's just say that if something shorts out, I'd rather it be for a different clan than my own. It could make my job as a doctor more difficult."

Iris snorted. "Fair point."

A familiar male voice came from inside the room. "I

thought you wanted answers, Iris? Or would you rather chat longer with Dr. Turner?"

Iris rolled her eyes, waved goodbye to the doctor, and headed into the room.

Antony sat at a small table, his hands steepled in front of him, wearing far more formal attire than normal —a gray suit, light blue shirt, and a dark blue tie.

The jacket highlighted his shoulders, and she resisted frowning. Had they always been that broad?

Her dragon hummed. *Yes. Imagine those long arms wrapped around us. His strong hands holding ours above our head as he fucked us.*

Stop it, dragon.

I only agreed to stop when wearing the thought translator. But you're not using it now.

Antony raised his eyebrows. "Just what was your dragon saying, I wonder? I can see your pulse racing in your neck."

Her beast spoke up. *I can make our heart go even faster. Like this.*

This time, Iris lay naked on a bed with Antony's head between her thighs, driving her crazy with his mouth and tongue and fingers.

Stop it.

No.

Needing to focus on anything but her dragon playing naked sex fantasies inside her head, she said, "Don't try to distract me. Dr. Turner said I can't go home to protect my clan, and I want to know why."

"There are many ways to protect your clan, Iris. And right now, working with me is the most helpful." He gestured toward the chair. "Sit. I have a lot to catch you up on before we leave."

She wanted to demand answers first and for him to stop being so vague all the time. And yet, he probably wouldn't like being challenged and it would only delay her learning anything. So Iris sat down, crossed her arms over her chest, and said, "So tell me, aye?"

"Right, well, let me give you the most important details, and we'll go from there."

And so he did: A human discovering a mass grave of dragon-shifters in their dragon forms; video footage of the grave online they were trying to get rid of; and lastly, only about half of the rogue dragon-shifters had been identified in the grave. Meaning some were buried elsewhere, or still alive, who knew where.

When he finished, Iris shook her head. "How the bloody hell did all of that happen in only five days?"

"It was already in motion when you first went to investigate. The initial autopsy findings show they were dead for two days before you flew to Cairngorms National Park. They're still working on a cause of death, but thanks to your blood tests right after your exposure, we suspect the same sort of gas killed them."

And if someone was willing to use it to mass murder once, what would stop them from using it against every dragon clan in the world?

Against her parents, her fellow Protectors, every dragon-shifter she'd ever met?

Would someone really try to rid the entire world of dragon-shifters?

Antony's voice was softer as he said, "I see you recognize the dangers. Which is why we need to stop whoever is doing this, as well as find out who is making it, and find a way to protect your kind from harm."

Right, focus on something you can do. "How? By using your super-secret team?"

"Partially. For the first time ever, my team is going to work with others. The DDA has seen to that."

She frowned. "Others who? Me?"

"You and the other head Protectors from Stonefire, Snowridge, Skyhunter, Northcastle, and Glenlough. Normally it would be Faye or Grant from Lochguard, but I'm aware of Faye's condition and her mate will be in no state of mind to focus. Plus, Cooper is busy handling the human protestors and a few other matters."

"Because of the news about the dragons vanishing."

She could only imagine the chaos. Poor Cooper.

But as much as she wanted to help him, someone needed to work with Antony's team.

Antony nodded. "Yes. Conspiracy theories are already springing up on the internet and social media about how the dragons are taking each other out. Oh, and how they'll try to conquer the humans next. The usual fear and irrational bullshit stirring people into a frenzy."

She muttered, "Just as we were getting things under control, too."

"That's the way of it, my dear. You squash two bugs and one more shows up."

"You have a pessimistic view of life, aye?"

"I have a reason to."

"Then why do any of this if it's pointless?"

He shook his head. "I never said it was pointless. There are individuals and groups that deserve to be squashed, no matter how difficult it might be."

Iris sensed there was more to his words than some boilerplate answer. However, before she could ask anything personal, Antony spoke again. "Back to the topic at hand. My team has access to resources you can't even begin to imagine. So this is your lucky day, Iris Mahajan, because you get to work with me and my toys."

She raised an eyebrow. "I wouldn't call working with you lucky."

He snorted. "Cheeky dragonwoman. But I like that about you, so don't ever change."

For a second, Antony's eyes searched hers, and she forgot about everything but the human male. How his brown eyes had flecks of gold in them. How his nose was slightly crooked, as if it'd been broken. The scar that peeked out from just under the cuff of his shirt.

Just how many scars and telltale signs did he have from his years with this secret team?

Her dragon spoke up. *Ask him to show us.*

Instead, Iris focused back on what she did best—her

job. "I'll find a way to endure your company. For now, you need to tell me everything you know, what resources we have, and when we can start investigating."

He nodded. "Focused. I like that."

Ignoring the rush of warmth at his praise, she growled, "Antony."

"Yes, yes, back to your assignment. You'll receive a packet with everything we know and be given time to study it after you finish recording your goodbye videos."

She blinked. "My what?"

He shrugged one shoulder. "All of my team members record goodbye messages before a mission, just in case. It's a bit morbid, but it helps give anyone you care about closure, if the worst happens."

Iris studied the human for a beat. "I would almost say you're sentimental."

He smiled wryly. "I can be. But it will also give you a clearer mind, knowing your parents will have something of you in case you die. Because I won't sugarcoat it—it's possible you will. Any dragon-shifter working on this assignment risks being exposed to the deadly gas. And whilst Dr. Turner is working on something to counteract it, she's not there yet. So I need you to answer me clearly: Do you understand the risks?"

"Aye, of course."

"Good." He took a file folder from his desk and handed it to her. "This has everything you need to know. I'll take you to the video recording room, and once you've finished, eaten, and had time to study your homework, we'll meet up with the others also working on this assignment."

Iris took the folder. "Good. I need to talk to the other Protectors and warn them about my experiences with the gas—the smell, the side effects, how quickly it works. The more information they have, the better."

"Yes, you'll meet with them, and everyone, later. Because even the human team members need as much information about the gas as you can give, in case they need to save their dragon-shifter partner. However, for the assignment itself, we're dividing up into teams of two. It's easier to stay in the shadows that way."

As he smiled at her, dread pooled in her belly. "I'm your partner, aren't I?"

"Yes, my dear. Each member of my secret team will pair with a dragon-shifter Protector, so it'll be just the two of us. And whilst Kai Sutherland has certainly proven himself over the years, you're the one I trust the most to watch my back." He winked. "Besides, I have the best gadgets to help us."

She was torn between snorting and rolling her eyes. "Boys and their toys. You're how old again?"

"All that matters is that I can be young at heart. Besides, I find humor works better than shouting and ordering people about."

"Are you saying I shout at people?"

"Do you?"

"Sometimes. But young Protectors need it, especially their inner dragons."

"Hmm, maybe in the future, you can help train them in the British Army. There's a major general who owes me a favor."

"Wait, I didn't ask for—"

He stood and waved a hand in dismissal. "That's the future. For now, we need to focus on finding out who created this bioweapon and determine if they sold it to one of your enemies or released it themselves. And fast. Because if not, there will be a lot of dead dragon-shifters."

Iris thought of her clan, of everyone laying lifeless, and she blurted, "Do you really think they'll try to commit genocide on my people?"

"I don't know. When people are angry or struggling, it's easier to blame someone else than to accept any responsibility themselves. And for far too many, they blame their troubles on the existence of dragon-shifters. It's preposterous, of course—there are many more humans in the world than dragons. And yet, I've been doing this long enough to know some people truly believe dragons are hoarding gold and jewels, laughing at the humans barely surviving, and are merely waiting to take over the world."

She studied Antony, looking for signs of weariness or cynicism or any other emotion to highlight his grim words. And yet, his expression was neutral. "How long have you been doing this, exactly?"

He waved a hand in dismissal. "That's for another time, my dear. You and I need to leave by nightfall.

That's only a few hours away, and we have far too much to do. So, follow me."

Even though she wanted to push, there were too many people relying on her to help Antony and the others, so she kept quiet.

However, Iris's mind buzzed as she followed Antony out of the room and down the hall. She itched to open the folder she carried, read everything, and get to work.

And yet, if this assignment really was as dangerous as Antony thought, she needed to leave something behind for her parents. Just in case.

Her dragon yawned and spoke up. *We'll make it through.*

Aye, I think so, too. But just in case, we'll take a few minutes to record a message. Mum will never get a son-in-law or any grandchildren, but I can at least give her a proper goodbye.

Her dragon fell silent, too silent. And she didn't like it.

But as they arrived at the room with the recording equipment, Iris focused on the message to her parents. And for good measure, she did one for her sort-of friends, Cooper and Brodie.

By the time she finished, she was more determined than ever to succeed. To date, this would be the most important mission of her life. And she wouldn't fuck it up, no matter what.

Chapter Eight

C ooper sat across from Finn Stewart, the Lochguard clan leader, and hoped the other Protectors could handle everything without him, given everything going on. However, if his clan leader had wanted an in-person meeting, then it had to be important.

Finn nodded in greeting and said, "I know you have a lot on your plate right now, aye? But Dr. McFarland finally learned the identity of the woman we found. And aye, I asked her to keep it quiet for the moment, even from you. Because the human's case is delicate and will require cooperation between clans."

He frowned, Finn's words piquing his interest. "Delicate, how?"

"Well, we're going to have to go behind the DDA's back."

Cooper sat up straighter at that. "Okay, now I'm curious. What's going on and who is this female?"

"She's been here before, with some of the children's plays, the human and dragon ones. Her name is Mariana Barlow."

He tried to place the female's face, but there had been quite a few humans at the event, and Cooper's focus during the plays had been to ensure everyone's safety.

But if she had come for the play, that meant she had at least one bairn. "I don't remember her, but what do you need?"

"She needs help, but I can't appear to be the one doing it. She needs to 'visit' Stonefire, but I don't want to know any of the details of how or who helps or any of that, so I can have plausible deniability with the DDA. But her ex-husband was the one who beat her and left her for dead, so she needs protection. The human government hadn't wanted to give her any, thinking her ex wasn't enough of a threat."

Cooper clenched his fingers into a fist. "Aye, I'll get her there. But if she was at the play, she has a bairn, right?"

"Aye, two. Her ex-husband threatened to flee with them to Northern Ireland, where his mother is from. I don't know if he's done that yet, but just in case, this situation gives me a chance to work with the new North-castle clan leader, Adrian Conroy."

Adrian had taken over the clan from Lorcan Todd

not too long ago. Cooper had met Adrian when he was still a Protector for the Northern Irish clan, but the male had shared little about himself. If he remembered right, Kaine Ferris had taken over the head Protector job. And even though he already had a mountain of responsibilities, Cooper said, "I can reach out to Northcastle's head Protector, too."

"No, no, don't worry about that. Like Iris and the others, he's on a mission that shall not be mentioned. For now, focus on Lochguard and picking someone you trust to watch over Mariana whilst she's here."

In other words, he needed to assign someone loyal to the clan who would do as asked and not share or brag about it later.

And Cooper knew exactly who to send.

He stood. "Aye, well, if that's all, I need to go assign Mariana Barlow a Protector, as well as prepare for any more protestors that might show up at our gates."

Finn shook his head. "Whilst I appreciate how the internet has helped the dragon clans grow closer, sometimes it's a pain in our arses when it stirs up chaos."

"At least the Dragon Knights are gone. If we can find a way to get rid of the dragon hunters, I think the majority of fear and hatred and propaganda will fade away."

"I hope you're right." Finn studied him a second before adding, "You haven't had the easiest time in charge, but I think you're doing a fine job, Cooper."

He snorted. "Right. Iris disappeared. Protestors are

trying to scale the walls. And a human female was left for dead just outside the clan's boundary. Brilliant work, isn't it?"

Finn shook his head. "No one could've foreseen all of this. Besides, by stepping up, you've saved Faye the stress. And for that, I thank you."

Faye was Finn's cousin. And since Faye's mother had taken in Finn after his parents died, they were all really close and more like siblings.

Cooper replied, "Faye is important to all of us, Finn. And I'll do my best. Although I'll need to bother them sometimes since I don't know everything."

"And that, right there, is why you'll be a good leader, aye? Don't be afraid to ask for help."

He nodded. "Aye, well, that won't be a problem. But I should go and talk to, er, someone about protecting the human female we found."

"Good lad. Keep it vague."

After saying their goodbyes, Cooper headed toward the Protector building. Even though Brodie wasn't due to start work for an hour, he knew the male would be there, like always.

His dragon yawned, waking up, and said, *He won't like being sent away.*

It's not being sent away. It's a high-priority mission. Besides, with Iris gone, he's the one I trust the most.

Is it that, or the fact he asks about the human female every day?

You really want to play matchmaker with everyone, don't you?

You won't go after any female, so I have to entertain myself somehow. Maybe you'll get tired of your hand soon and go after her.

I'm not having this discussion again. I see Brodie ahead. Let's give him his assignment.

And as Brodie quickly accepted the job without protest, Cooper wondered if his dragon was right. Maybe Brodie and Mariana would hit it off.

Although that would be a long road, given what had just happened to Mariana. But if anyone could win over a hurt, somewhat damaged female, it would be Brodie MacNeil.

An hour after Iris finished recording her goodbye videos, she headed toward the conference room where everyone working on the mission should be.

While no one would tell her the exact location of the facility she'd been inside during her recovery, it took security to the next level. Even the room where she'd studied the folder of information had been mostly empty save for a desk, chair, and light. Someone had brought her a sandwich and some tea, but it had been served with paper dishes and plastic cutlery. Almost as if they expected her to break a mug and use the shards as a weapon.

Her dragon spoke up. *Maybe not us, but someone must've done it. Eventually, they might trust us. He might trust us.*

Not again. The mission is more important than you getting some sex, dragon.

Aye, I know. And I won't risk anyone's life. But if we just happen to get trapped somewhere, alone, and need to pass the time...

Quiet. Or I'll put you in a mental maze.

Her beast harrumphed. *Fine. For now. But I mean it —if there's an opportunity and it won't endanger anyone, I'm taking it.*

Not wanting to argue, Iris opened the door of the conference room and walked inside.

Five Protectors sat along one side of a long table, with an empty seat at the end, most likely saved for her. A human female Iris recognized—Alice Darby, although she'd dyed her hair a less noticeable brown now—sat at the foot of the table. The side opposite the Protectors had a mixture of humans and dragons she'd never met.

And, of course, Antony sat at the head of the table.

She addressed the male. "Why didn't you tell me everyone was already here and waiting for me?"

Antony replied, "I needed Dr. Turner's final blood results before I could summon you. And you're completely cleared now, Iris. So sit down and let's get started."

She bit her tongue, not wanting to seem petty in front of her fellow Protectors, and nodded at Kai from

Stonefire as she took the empty seat. She'd worked with him many times over the years and trusted him the most in the room.

She wondered if the other head Protectors would accept her or not. Female Protectors were becoming more common, but some males still had old-fashioned ideas.

However, before she could greet anyone, Antony spoke again. "We may not all trust each other yet, but if this mission is to be a success, then we need to share information and not be afraid to ask for help. I won't have egos getting in the way—you're all equal for this assignment. And if you can't accept that, then leave now."

Everyone glanced around, but no one left.

Not that Iris could blame them. For a human, Antony knew how to thread his voice with dominance like a dragon clan leader. Her dragon rumbled, but thankfully stayed quiet, no doubt wanting to make some innuendo about him in bed.

After a few more beats, Antony continued. "Right, then let's get this meeting started. First up is our DDA liaison, Alice Darby."

The human female snorted. "Liaison is a bit of a stretch. But yes, I'm to formally report back to the DDA Director even though I'm not your typical DDA employee. Antony recruited me because, after making some foolish mistakes as a teenager, I managed to hide from several DDA-like agencies for ten years. And during that time, I learned about the black markets and groups who wanted to kill dragon-shifters, hoping I could find a way to destroy them."

Alice was referring to the illegal sale of dragon's blood, which had extraordinary healing abilities. However, it usually only ended up on the black market if someone had drained a dragon of blood, killing them.

Kaine Ferris from Northcastle frowned. "We've been trying to stop the sale of dragon's blood on the black markets for years. Any information could've helped, so why haven't you shared this before?"

"I have, with Antony and his team. I was ordered to keep it quiet from anyone else."

Iris's gaze shot to the human male's, but he didn't so much as blink before saying, "There will be a lot of surprises in the coming days, so you'd better get used to it. As you recall, the rogue dragon-shifters have been a problem for years now. And since there are sympathetic clan members in every dragon clan, we had to be extra careful and not risk this information getting out."

Iris asked, "Who is the 'we' you're talking about?"

Antony shook his head. "For now, let's just focus on the mission and then maybe you can learn more about who I work for."

Just as Kaine was about to ask something else, one of Antony's team members jumped in, his accent Northern Irish. "You have secrets too, Ferris, so don't play all high-and-mighty." Kaine's gaze shot to the unknown dragon-man, and he continued, "But just like I won't reveal how there are quite a few humans living on Northcastle without permission, you won't share any of the information discussed here."

Kaine didn't even attempt to look sheepish. "You're from Northern Ireland and a dragon-shifter, and yet I have no fucking idea who you are."

"I'm Joseph Doyle, at your service. And all I'll say is my father was human, and my parents were shunned. So I grew up on the lam."

Until recently, few human males had been allowed to mate and live with female dragon-shifters. If a female dragon had fallen in love or found her true mate in a human, her only choices had been to leave her clan or reject them to stay with her people.

Since Scotland had a splinter clan, Seahaven, full of human and dragon mated pairs who'd been kicked off Lochguard in the past—in the time before Finn Stewart —Iris asked, "Is there a smaller clan in Northern Ireland, then, where your parents and others went to live?"

Joseph replied, "Maybe I'll answer that in time."

She was about to ask another question when Antony spoke up. "You all will have time later to get to know each other, especially with your assigned partners for this assignment. Steering us back on track, let me share your pairings now. Iris will be with me. Kaine, you'll be working with Joseph. Kai, you'll be with Trina. Wren, you're with Christopher. Killian, you'll be with Kerry. And Robin, you'll be with Gavin. The dragon-dragon pairings will need to be more careful. Because, sadly, I don't have more humans to work with right now."

Trina spoke up. "Three died a few months ago and they haven't been replaced yet."

Iris studied the human female with black hair, dark brown eyes, and light tan skin. "I've seen you before, haven't I? Weren't you an informant first and then showed up later during a mission?"

"Yes, I helped with Jake Swift."

The human male had been kidnapped, and as he'd fallen in love with a female dragon on Lochguard, they'd rescued him. But even so, there was something familiar about her she couldn't place, almost like she reminded Iris of someone.

Antony's voice garnered her attention. "I'll go over your individual assignments in private. But first, Iris is going to tell us everything she can about experiencing the dangerous gas and living to tell the tale."

All eyes turned toward her, but she didn't blink. She'd taught flight maneuvers to Protectors and teenagers for years and didn't mind public speaking. "Well, here's what I noticed..."

She went through the smell, the dizziness, the lack of strength, and anything else she could remember. After the others asked a few clarifying questions, Antony stood and said without preamble, "Time to go over assignments. Kai and Trina, you're first. Come with me."

Once they'd left, Iris glanced at Joseph, who seemed

the most chatty of Antony's team, and asked, "Is this standard procedure, to keep the assignments secret?"

"Aye. That way, no amount of torture can get it out of you."

The male spoke as if he knew from experience.

The female dragon-shifter from Antony's team, Kerry Penrose, spoke up in her English accent, one Iris couldn't place. "You're the lucky one, though, Iris. Antony has the best of everything. Not because he doesn't want to share, but over the years, the gear and gadgets have been designed specifically for him."

Iris noticed her opening. "Just how long has Antony been doing this job?"

Kerry shook her head. "I honestly have no idea. Decades, I think? But I do wonder how Antony's done this job for so long. I've been here for two years, and I'm already wondering when I can see less action."

The human male, Gavin Edwards, snorted. "Says the dragon-shifter who'd be bored off her arse if she had a desk job."

Kerry gave him a double-finger salute. "You're only saying that because you're jealous. You've never beaten me in the qualifying trials to steal my job and be promoted."

"I've come close. And since I'm human, that means you're losing your touch, Kerry."

She narrowed her eyes, and as they bickered—in a sort of code that Iris couldn't decipher—the human male named Christopher spoke to her in an accent she couldn't identify. "Ignore them. They've wanted to fuck since the first day but are too afraid, in case he's her true mate."

Gavin and Kerry both stalled their conversations to state, "Not true."

Joseph leaned back in his chair. "I've bet on the pair of you, but I won't tell you which way."

Before Gavin or Kerry could say anything else, Antony returned without Kai or Trina. "Killian and Kerry, you're next."

Joseph pumped his fist. "Huzzah. Now we'll get some peace and quiet."

Kerry glared. "Fuck you, Joseph."

The male merely chuckled. Iris kept trying to find an opening to ask Joseph some questions, but the others grew chatty and she never had a chance. And as the numbers dwindled in the room, Iris realized she'd be last, meaning she could only ask Antony for answers and hope he didn't hold back.

Her dragon spoke up. *You're impatient. You knew he was our partner for this, so why are you surprised that we're last?*

Not surprised, but he could've given me some materials to study whilst we waited. Something instead of sitting here, listening to gossip and me trying to figure out if I can jump in to ask some relevant questions.

We don't even know what our assignment is yet, aye?

Just enjoy the downtime because soon we probably won't have any.

Iris begrudgingly did her best to listen to the others and learn what she could. Eventually, she was the last person in the room. By the time Antony came for her, she itched to jump up and demand where they were going and what they would be doing.

However, determined not to let the human get to her again, she calmly asked, "Where are we going?"

"The Peak District. I'll explain when we arrive. For now, we need to change and get our gear." He gestured toward the door. "Come on."

As they exited the room and walked down yet another corridor, Iris clenched and unclenched her fingers. Antony had bloody well better tell her about their assignment soon. She hated being kept in the dark. He was probably doing it on purpose.

Her dragon spoke up. *Where's your legendary patience?*

Before she could reply, Antony finally guided her into a room full of tactical gear and weapons. Her jaw dropped as she looked from the walls covered with weapons to the various mannequins wearing protective gear.

Many of the items she couldn't even identify, let alone know what they did.

Antony said, "Go on, my dear. Take a look around whilst I get a few things you'll need."

She barely noticed him leave as she went to inspect the trove of treasures.

And for the first time in her life, Iris wanted to horde it all and be like one of those dragons in the human fairytales.

Chapter Nine

Antony returned to his gadget room and watched as Iris inspected the various weapons and protective gear. She kept reaching for something, her eyes wide with wonder, before retreating again.

Some women wanted candy and flowers. But it seemed Iris Mahajan preferred night scopes, tranquilizer guns, and signal jammers.

Not that it was a negative. He was the same. Although he wondered how she'd react to flowers and him cooking for her.

She must've noticed his return because she swirled around, holding a prototype stun gun that could shoot a beam of electricity, like right out of a sci-fi show, and asked, "Are you always so creepy?"

"If you mean do I always sneak up on people and

hide in the shadows, then the answer is mostly yes." She opened her mouth to ask questions he didn't really want to answer, so he strode toward her and said, "You'll need these, when in your human form. They're special contacts that will hide your flashing dragon eyes. Not even an eye scanner can detect you wearing them."

"Let me guess—you have a secret army of dragon-shifters living in London, Manchester, and loads of other big cities, ready in case of attack."

His lips twitched as he handed her the contact case. "Something like that."

"You're always annoyingly vague, aye?"

"Well, do you spill secrets every chance you get?"

"You don't have to spill secrets to give a little bit of detail. Because if we're in a life-or-death situation and you're still vague, it could kill us both. And I'd prefer not to die for stupid reasons, aye?"

"I would never willingly put you in danger. Ever."

The fierceness of his tone made her blink. "Okay."

Her gaze searched his, and Antony wondered how much she could see of the real him. Part of him wanted to drop the act and merely tease her, woo her, challenge her for fun in a sparring match, only for him to pin her down and maybe kiss her.

He nearly frowned. Why was he so bloody drawn to this dragonwoman? Especially since she always seemed so skeptical of him.

Not wanting to think of the why, he took out a small device and held it up. "Before we leave, I need to chip you. And before you get upset, we all have them. They can even survive a dragon shifting."

She eyed the small gun-like device. "Wouldn't your enemy be able to find the chips and disable them?"

"Ah, but you see, our technology is better and decades more advanced than anything the public has access to. Almost nothing can deactivate it, and it's nearly as hard to tell it's even there." He gestured around the room. "Most of this could start a war, if other countries knew about it. Only those I trust have access."

She searched his gaze. "And why do you trust me so much? All we ever do is fight or argue."

"You helped save my brother more than once, when he got distracted on a dig. Max trusts you, which means I do, too."

His younger brother loved archaeology and history above all else. And while he'd worked with Antony for a short while on some secret assignments, Max became too easily distracted. So, after being sworn to secrecy, Antony had released his brother from his team.

However, Max used his training under Antony all the time, and had given his report of Iris long before Antony had ever revealed himself to her.

She cleared her throat. "Aye, well, there's still so much I don't know about you, so I can't say I trust you as much."

He should make light of her comment, tease her, and distract her with everything in the room.

And yet, his years of training faded as he blurted, "I like to paint."

Fuck, why had he shared that?

Iris's brows drew together. "What kind of painting? Because if you say nudes and ask me to pose, I'm going to roll my eyes and walk away."

"No, no nudes. Just forget I said anything."

She walked closer and placed a hand on his arm. Heat flared at her touch, sending electricity throughout his body.

But Iris looked unaffected and merely asked, "What kind of paintings?"

He cleared his throat. "You'll laugh."

"I promise not to."

While vows were more iron-clad for dragon-shifters, Antony decided to risk it. "Pets."

She blinked. "Pets?"

"I can't have one with my line of work. So I paint them instead and leave the canvases around London for people to find."

He waited for her to laugh. Because, really, it was ridiculous. Antony was privy to the most classified information in the country, commanded a team with few limits, and could kill a man before he even knew of his presence.

And yet, he enjoyed painting cats and dogs and birds in silly situations and watching as people found them. Usually, they smiled or laughed. The ones who destroyed them often had bad luck later on.

Completely by coincidence, of course.

Iris still had her hand on his arm and squeezed. "That's kind of sweet, aye? I can't have pets, either, because of my job. But I do have..."

She looked away, and Antony raised a hand to gently force her gaze back. "Have what? If I can tell you about painting puppies, you can tell me anything."

After biting her bottom lip for a few seconds—which Antony struggled not to stare at—she answered, "I had a cat as a wee lass, and later, once she passed, I got a stuffed animal that looks like her. I still have it."

"If you have a picture of your cat, I can paint something for you."

She frowned. "You're not going to tease me about it? Only one person ever found out about my stuffed animal, and he never let me live it down."

"Tell me his name and he'll never bother you again."

"I can't tell if you're serious or joking."

"Oh, I'm serious. No one should make you embarrassed for loving someone, be it a pet or person."

Antony had gone through that with his late fiancée. His colleagues had teased him about being smitten, and being young and stupid, he'd taken risks. Unnecessary risks that had ended up getting Lisa killed.

Iris's voice snapped him back to the present. "What were you just thinking about? Because pain briefly flashed in your eyes."

Bloody hell. Did he forget all of his training around this dragonwoman?

His phone chimed, and he quickly took it out to check. "Right, memory lane will have to wait. We need to leave in the next ten minutes or we won't arrive at our destination whilst it's still dark. Come on. There's a changing room with some stuff for you next door."

He turned and walked off to the side. Part of him wanted Iris to push and ask him uncomfortable questions about his past, and the other part wanted her to drop it.

And so when she remained quiet and eventually went into the changing room as instructed, he wondered why he felt a little bit sad.

Get it together. Emotions were nothing but trouble. Be it pride, love, or fear—any of those could get someone killed.

With that thought, Antony recited focusing exercises inside his mind, to get it together. By the time Iris emerged wearing protective gear that looked like any other pair of jeans and sweater, Antony merely nodded and motioned for her to follow. He needed to get to the Peak District before sunrise, and he'd be damned if he missed the window of arrival because of a woman.

As soon as they were on the road and Iris had been allowed to take off her blindfold—no doubt to hide the exact location of the facility—she studied Antony's profile. Earlier, he'd seemed so...vulnerable. When embarrassment had flashed across his features while talking about his paintings, it'd made her pause and blurt out something personal, too.

Why had she told him about Fluffy the Cat?

And why, oh why, had she bothered to touch him? She could still feel the strong, lean muscles of his arm beneath her fingers.

Her dragon spoke up. *You remember because you want him to touch us some more. Especially after learning he's not the arsehole-y superhero of ice like you thought before.*

I still can't believe he paints pets. And then leaves them for people to find.

You have a stuffed animal cat. It's not that hard to imagine.

But he's so...snobby. And acts like he's better than everyone.

You, more than anyone, know how important it is to keep up appearances and façades.

During her year with the British Army—which all future Protectors had to serve—Iris had tried to make friends with the humans. She'd even thought herself in love with one.

Until her world had come tumbling down.

Antony's voice brought her back to the present. "If you take a picture with your phone, it'll last longer."

"What the bloody hell are you talking about now?"

"You're staring. And have been for at least ten minutes."

"Maybe I'm trying to learn your tells, or any other kind of information, since you won't share anything with me."

He raised an eyebrow but kept his eyes on the road. "I will as soon as we arrive. I told you that."

"Why, though? It's dangerous to go into a situation blind."

He glanced briefly at her, his expression unreadable. "I have sentries posted along our route, watching and monitoring us. If something happens to me, one of them will find you within minutes and whisk you away to safety."

"I'm not a bloody damsel in distress. So stop treating me like one, aye?"

"You could be a seven-foot-tall man armed to the teeth, and I'd act exactly the same way."

"I've heard that bullshit before."

"Ah, during your time with the army?"

She blinked. "What do you know?"

He tapped the side of his nose. "More than you'd like me to, I reckon. And before you get mad or shout, just know I looked up the backgrounds of *all* the Protectors working with me, not just you. So there's no need to be defensive with me, my dear. If you weren't amazing at your job, you wouldn't be here, end of story. I value both my work and those I protect far too much to hire less than the best. I don't care if they have a dick or not. If anything, it's usually a negative."

Rather than focus on Antony praising her, she blurted, "Why?"

His lips twitched. "It takes a lot of time and training to deprogram the expected privilege most men have since it won't help them in a life-or-death situation where the other side will kill whoever they meet."

"If only they did that in the army, or at least those who work with the dragon-shifters. I can't speak to the human-only units."

"In the military, even the human side, you're part of a group. Still, it's hard to get rid of ego. Which is something I won't tolerate in my most trusted team members."

She raised an eyebrow. "I find it hard to believe you lack an ego."

"None of us do. But some individuals let it rule them, and it ends up getting people killed. In my experience, men, especially, don't like to admit they're wrong. I have to test them early. Because if they can't learn from their mistakes, then they're unworthy and a waste of my time."

Interesting. Antony Holbrook seemed to understand the faults of males more than most. She asked, "So how do you test them? Or is that another secret of yours?"

He shrugged. "Not really. It depends on the individual. Most of the time, I ask about something they did poorly in the past and see how they react. Those who own up to their mistakes get more points than those who try to explain them away. The ones who outright deny it, well, they get a shot of a short-term memory loss drug and don't remember a thing about me or that facility we left."

Iris frowned. "So you would've used that memory loss drug on me if I'd refused to work with you?"

"Oh, I knew you would accept the offer, my dear. So it never crossed my mind."

"To save or protect my clan, I'd do anything."

"Exactly. But you also crave the challenge. You don't strike me as someone who'd settle for being a mere Protector your whole life, without the chance to lead. And since Faye and Grant are quite young, they'll probably be in charge for a while. This is your chance to impress me and maybe earn a permanent place on my team."

Ignoring the thrill of being able to carry out missions regularly, Iris drawled, "Impress you, aye?"

"Aye, impress me," he mimicked in her accent. One that sounded as if he'd been Scottish his whole life.

"So now you do accents. Just how many skills do you have?"

He snorted. "My mimicry comes from doing impressions as a child. At one point, I thought about becoming an actor or to even do comedy."

"How the bloody hell did you go from wanting to be a comedian to being a James Bond on steroids?"

"I'm flattered you think I'm like James Bond. But, in

actuality, he's an idiot compared to what me and my team can do."

"What was that about ego?" she drawled.

"It's not ego when it's the truth, my dear. How many times did Bond get distracted by a pretty woman? I mean, honestly, I would've kicked him off my team after the first time."

"True. I stopped watching after one film because I started shouting at the screen and people got angry."

He laughed. "I would love to see that. Maybe we should have a team-building exercise where we watch a James Bond film and point out the flaws."

"Whilst that would be entertaining, I'd rather focus on finding out who created that gas, is spreading it around, and who murdered all those dragon-shifters. Even if they were traitors, they didn't deserve to die like that."

"Some of them did, though. A few were leaking information to Simon Bourne and his cronies."

She sat up straighter. "What?"

Simon Bourne was the leader of the dragon hunters, who hated that dragon-shifters had any rights. His people only wanted dragons so they could drain them of blood and sell it on the black market. In their ideal world, they'd keep dragons in pens, drugged and treated as nothing more than a resource they wanted to control.

Antony replied, "It's true. One of the worst offenders from the clanless dragon group was Grant's father, Michael."

"Wait, how? He was captured and transferred to the DDA's care years ago."

Michael McFarland had formerly betrayed Lochguard and truly believed dragons were superior to humans and should rule over them. The thought of him working with Simon Bourne, a human, didn't make sense.

Antony replied, "This isn't common knowledge, but he and a few others escaped from a DDA prison about a year ago."

"What? How could you not tell us about that? Both Grant and Chase have bairns now, and given how their mates are dragon-shifters, I wouldn't put it past Michael to kidnap and raise his grandchildren 'the right way' in his mind, meaning without humans."

"I'm aware of his anti-human sentiments. But we couldn't risk sharing this information with anyone but a select few. If news got out about dragon-shifters escaping from DDA prisons, what do you think would happen?"

While Iris wanted to strangle Antony for keeping this information secret—and for how much it might've hurt her clan—she took a deep breath and tried to think about it rationally. Part of her job relied on her being able to control her emotions to focus.

After a few seconds, she replied, "If the news got out, then both humans and dragons would've panicked. But you could've at least told Grant. He's loyal, wouldn't share the information with anyone but his mate, and could better protect his daughter and nephews."

"Perhaps. However, I have things in hand. For now. I may have to talk to Grant soon, anyway, since his uncle Roderick was one of the bodies found in the mass grave."

Iris remembered Roderick McFarland. He'd never been a nice person and had caused her clan some pain, but he still didn't deserve to be murdered. No, he should've faced justice instead.

Eager to learn as much as possible before Antony closed himself off again, she asked, "Can you stop dropping information little by little and just tell me who from Lochguard was found in the grave? If I know who's still alive, I might be able to shed some light about how they'll act or react since we have files on all of them. In fact, I bet all the clans have files and could share. And since you've recruited the head Protectors for this set of missions, that must mean you trust them. At least somewhat, aye?"

He glanced at her, but Iris couldn't read his expression. Part of her admired him for his control, and another part wished he'd relax a little more around her.

Her dragon snorted. *And why is that?*

Shush, dragon.

Why? With the contacts in, he can't even tell we're talking, aye? Actually, that could be fun—to flash sexy scenes in your head, make you hot and bothered, and Antony would think it's you and not me.

Don't even think about it.

Oh, calm down. I wouldn't embarrass you that far. Although, I think you want him to loosen up around us because you're curious. Curious enough to want to know the man behind the façade. Especially since he treats us as an equal and not lesser because of our gender or skin color.

"Iris?"

A hand touched her thigh, and electricity raced through her body. Her gaze met Antony's, and he frowned before looking back at the road. "I asked you a question three times, and you never answered. Maybe I should've waited to give you the special contacts until later, so I can tell if you're chatting with your dragon or ignoring me."

His hand lingered, and for a second, he stroked her inner thigh.

But in the next second, he snatched his hand back, as if he'd been burned. "Pardon. I shouldn't touch you."

Her dragon hummed. *Yes, he should.*

Iris ignored her beast and cleared her throat. "If you vow to never touch me, then what if I fall and to save me, you need to grab my hand?"

"You know what I mean."

"Aye, but it's fun to tease you."

He smiled, glanced at her, and back to the road. "I like you with your metaphorical hair down, Iris. I think you don't let down your guard enough."

"And you do?"

"Touché. But if we're to work together, we should probably stop putting up masks at every opportunity when we're alone. Deal?"

She studied his profile again. Her gut said this was a bad idea. She already sort of liked him. And if she relaxed, and he still teased and flirted and touched her? She might be stupid enough to open her heart again.

And yet, she pictured Antony leaving a picture with a kitten for a little girl to find on the tube in London, and she instantly wanted to know what else he did, outside of his job.

Or how he'd managed to keep his sense of humor and sanity intact after doing this type of work for so long.

She'd just have to ensure she didn't let him in too much.

Her dragon sighed but remained quiet.

Iris nodded and answered, "Aye, deal. I'd shake hands, but I'd rather you focus on the road. Single track roads can be a pain to drive."

"I rather like them because there are fewer arseholes around. Yes, some people don't know the rules about who pulls over when they meet another car coming the opposite way. But considering the people I've had to face over the years, and some of the jobs I've had to carry out, it pales in comparison."

This was her chance to know him better. So she asked, "What was your first assignment? Or maybe your most memorable? Unless you can't share either without killing me?"

"I would never do anything to endanger you, my dear."

"So, does that mean your entire past is a secret?"

He gripped the steering wheel a little tighter. "A lot of it, but not all."

"Then tell me about one of your most memorable missions."

Antony remained quiet for over a minute, and Iris wondered if she'd pushed too hard.

But then he said quietly, "The most memorable is the one that got my fiancée killed."

Chapter Ten

A ntony probably shouldn't have said that. And the longer Iris sat in stunned silence, the more he cursed his mouth and his inability to keep quiet around the dragonwoman.

And yet, there was something about her, something that made him want to confide, that he couldn't resist. Maybe it was because he'd been doing this job for too long and was losing his edge. Or maybe, just maybe, it wasn't something he could control.

Maybe he was her true mate.

Since female dragon-shifters couldn't tell who their true mate was like the male ones could, and a kiss could set off a mate-claim frenzy, Antony should try harder to avoid getting close to her. Because if he was hers and he kissed her on the lips, he would either have to run away or agree to the frenzy and sleep with Iris until she was pregnant.

While deep down he wished to have a child some-day, now was not the time. Not to mention he didn't even know what Iris wanted for her future.

Besides, even if she wanted him, Antony had a lot of enemies. Ones that maybe didn't know his identity yet but might one day. And then they'd go after anyone he cared about.

And he refused to risk another woman getting killed because of him.

As he tried to think of a way to brush off the comment, Iris asked, "What happened?"

He glanced at her, and at the curiosity in her eyes, he didn't think he could deny her. "It's not a pretty tale, my dear. Do you really want to hear it? Because at the end you might despise me and then I'll have to send you home. I can't work with someone who won't have my back."

"I'd rather know than not. That way, I can be better prepared for what might happen, aye?"

As he turned off the single-track road onto a regular one, he contemplated how much he should tell her.

However, the more he thought about it, the more he realized that if he didn't tell her everything, Iris would know and then never trust him.

Better to get it out and see if she wants to run or not, right, old chap?

"Right, well, I need to back up a little bit, to before the mission started. Much like you, I served time with the British Army. Nearly eight years, in fact, before they recruited me for the department I'm in now. However, I was still young then, just twenty-four, and rather full of myself for being recruited at all. Most of the time, I hid it well, and I was known to be jovial and yet a closed book at the same time."

"Much like now, then."

"Yes. As much as I've tried, my sense of humor is around for good. But back to when I entered the Wicked Security team—the full title is Human-Dragon Wicked Security Department—and my first real mission. The training lasted months, and over twenty years ago, it was very much men trying to be macho and outdo each other. I've tried to change some of that over the years— machismo gets people killed—but I wasn't yet enlightened.

"The training wasn't a huge deal, but the others saw me as somewhat 'burdened' because I was one of the few with a fiancée. Normally, Wicked Security team members are single and unattached. However, my ability to strategize and memorize large amounts of information quickly was too valuable to pass up. And when approached, I said I would only join if I could stay with Lisa. She would think I worked a regular desk job with the government, but I wouldn't have to give her up. Not perfect, but I loved her and couldn't imagine life without her."

In retrospect, he'd been selfish, trying to have his cake and eat it too. There was a reason most members of Wicked Security didn't have partners—because they were weaknesses who could be targeted. The few who did have families either retired to desk work and analysis, or married other team members who could protect themselves.

Not for the first time, Antony wished he'd chosen Lisa over the job. Even if they'd eventually broken up, she wouldn't have died because of his choices. Ones made without her knowing just how risky his life would become.

Iris's voice brought him back to the present. "What happened, Antony? Because if guilt still flashes across your face, it makes me wonder how badly you fucked up, aye?"

The corner of his mouth kicked up. "Succinctly put, my dear. I fucked up. Massively."

"And if you think I'm going to let you stop there, you're mad."

He glanced at her. "Demanding, aren't you?"

She raised an eyebrow. "You have no idea."

He laughed, despite everything. "Well, then let me continue, lest I stir up your temper." She opened her mouth to protest, but Antony knew he needed to get this all out as quickly as possible. So he spoke before her. "After taking the job and finishing my training, things went well for a while. With my better salary, Lisa and I had started to make plans. And once they transferred me to Greater Manchester from London, we even started looking at homes. We'd barely moved into our new place before everything went horribly wrong."

Even now, he remembered Lisa scouring the charity shops to decorate their small two-bedroom attached row house. Her biggest prize had been an old pitcher she'd turned into a vase.

One that had ended up smashed on the floor.

Mentally shaking himself, Antony focused on the road and, keeping his voice steady as he said, "My first assignment involved the early version of today's dragon hunters. They were a bit less organized back then, and they worked more like gangs with specific territory than the organized entity they are now. I would use my mimicry skill to pretend I was Mancunian born and raised, watch them from the shadows, and eventually try to get recruited."

Iris asked, "So you worked undercover with the dragon hunters?"

"Barely. You're getting ahead of me, my dear. Patience." The dragonwoman rolled her eyes, and he smiled. "Back to my story, unless you're bored?"

"No. No way. Continue."

"Right, well, I eventually ended up passing the dragon hunter recruitment test given to me. And before you ask, I had to do something I'm not proud of—beat up a dragonman until he was unconscious and draw a vial of blood. With new technology, they were trying to see if they could use dragon's blood if the shifter was in their human form. While the answer was no, it was the only way to get them to trust me." He glanced at Iris. "Later, I ensured that dragonman got whatever favors he needed, without ever knowing it was me. You might know him—Bronx Wells."

She nodded. "Aye, I've met him. His brother, Hudson, mated Lachlan MacKintosh's sister, Sarah. But Bronx still doesn't know it was you that beat him up?"

He shook his head. "No. And it's best he never does. Even though I haven't apologized to him, I've made it up to him several times over, even if he doesn't know it. I still watch over him and Percy, just in case they need my help again."

Percy Smith, now Wells, was a former prisoner that had been assaulted and isolated, raised without knowing how to be a dragon-shifter. She'd eventually mated Bronx Wells and now had a child.

But Antony hurting a random dragon-shifter wasn't even the worst part of his tale. He steeled himself for Iris to rail at him.

However, Iris didn't shout or scold but instead crossed her arms over her chest and replied, "Aye, well, I won't tell him. I understand having to do things you don't like for the greater good. But getting back to your story—you passed their test and became a dragon hunter. How does this tie into your fiancée being killed?"

He gripped the steering wheel tighter. "I'm getting to that. I had to meet with my contact from Wicked Security every week. He wanted to retire and was training his replacement, who was a dragon-shifter I'd always disliked. The replacement bragged about everything, and being young, I kept trying to prove I was better than him.

"So later, when his mentor had to take a call and we were alone, he taunted me about not getting any information yet. And because it was taking so long, my fiancée had to be lonely and maybe he should try to steal her away from me since dragon-shifters took better care of their women. And even though his mentor returned, and the dragonman remained silent for the rest of the meeting, his challenge lingered. So I started taking risks and ignoring precautions—I wanted to find out where they drained the dragons of their blood. And just when I thought I'd figured it all out, I was caught."

Taking a second, Antony kept the memories locked away. He'd been tortured a few times in his life, and yet, he still had nightmares whenever he tried to sort through the memories.

And with everything going on, he couldn't afford to have any.

Iris asked, "They hurt you, didn't they?"

His gaze shot to hers. "Yes."

She nodded. "I was captured by a group of young dragon hunters briefly, once. I escaped, but not before they drugged me with something to keep me from shifting and then proceeded to beat the crap out of me."

Anger shot through him. "Who?"

"Over the years, I've captured most of them and turned them over to the DDA. One of them, though, works closely with Simon Bourne now. So if you want to help me take care of him, we need to take down the dragon hunters entirely."

"Give me his name now."

She raised an eyebrow. "You sound like a growly dragonman, aye?"

"The dragon hunters have hurt too many people over the years. They deserve to be taken down, and some of them need to be punished."

"Is that something else your little group does, then? You fly under the radar and don't obey the law?"

"We do. Mostly. There are some gray areas, but even those have limits."

She studied him a second before saying, "You want me to ask about the limits and forget about your first mission. But that won't work, aye?"

"Caught that, did you, my dear? Well done. It usually works with the other members of my team."

"Antony, stop stalling and tell me the rest. You said you would."

"I did, didn't I?" He sighed. "Well, back to me being tortured. I survived without saying a word. However, I mentioned Lisa's name in my sleep one night and it was enough. They dumped me outside our place, and I went inside. Where I found her..."

Seeing her lifeless body on the ground, naked, with her throat slit, was something he'd never forget.

Iris laid a hand on his arm, bringing him back to the present. "It's okay. You don't have to go into the details."

He shook his head. "No, I should. Just so you fully understand what you're getting into with me."

"Then tell me."

After taking a deep breath, Antony kept his eyes on the road and said, "They'd raped her and then slit her throat. After that, they wrote a message on the wall in her blood: *She's dead because of you. You're next.*"

Dead because of you. For months, the words had haunted him. Only through the strict training and routine of Wicked Security had he pulled out of the dark, dark place he'd been in.

An image of Lisa, smiling at him and kissing him hello when he returned from work, flashed into his mind. Such a sweet soul had been snuffed out too early. A bright future, full of love, extinguished because he'd been a selfish bastard.

His old guilt crashed down over him, and Antony struggled to pull over to the side of the road. Once the engine was off, he leaned his head against the headrest, closed his eyes, and did his best to pull himself together. He was close, so close, to the beginning of the end of the dragon hunters. And he bloody well wouldn't let them win, all these years later.

Defeating them was the only way to avenge his first love.

And yet, it was harder than usual for him to push aside the memories. He'd made a fatal mistake by letting Iris in, even a little.

He'd just have to try harder at keeping his distance.

But then Iris took his hand.

As soon as Antony had stopped on the side of the road, closed his eyes, and leaned his head back against the headrest, Iris snapped out of her shock and reached for his hand. He tried to bat her away, but she was stubborn and eventually gripped his fingers in hers.

The fight drained out of him, and she tried to imagine finding someone she loved, like her parents, lying on the floor with their throats slit and a message written on the wall in their blood.

Right here, right now, Antony was just a male. Not the bloke who teased her or irritated her or made her heart race. Just a miserable human who blamed himself for the past.

Her dragon spoke up. *He needs us right now. Don't fight it.*

Given how Antony now clung to her hand like his life depended on it, Iris couldn't deny it. *I'm not sure what I can do.*

Yes, you do.

"Antony."

He rubbed his free hand down his face. "It'll take me some time to coordinate a ride home to your clan. But I just need a few minutes first."

"What the bloody hell are you talking about?"

His eyes shot open, and he turned toward her. "You can't still want to work with me, Iris."

"And here I thought you weren't the type of male to tell me what I should think, aye?"

His brows came together. "You can't be rejoicing that I was a stupid young man who let my ego and pride get in the way and kill a sweet, innocent woman."

"If I were celebrating that, then I'd worry about myself, aye?"

"Iris," he growled.

She gripped his hand tighter. "Look, we all do stupid shite sometimes. And whilst aye, yours was more extreme, it's done. We can't change the past, only work on doing better in the future. And seeing as how you've dedicated over twenty years to this Wicked Security team, I think you've been doing the best you can."

He finally managed to shake her hand off and instead gripped the steering wheel. "Maybe. But if I'm not careful, they could murder you, too."

"Look at me, Antony Holbrook." He did, and she continued, "I never knew your Lisa, but did she have training with the British Army? Spend over a decade working with a dragon security team? Face dragon hunters and Dragon Knights and live to tell the tale?"

"No, but—"

"I'm not done. I can protect myself. Aye, sometimes I need help, and I ask for it, as much as I don't like it. But I've faced a lot of dangers since I was eighteen, and I've made it to nearly thirty. There's always a risk I won't survive to the next mission, and I accept that. But I push on because protecting my clan and my parents is everything. However, if you doubt that, if you don't believe in me, then maybe we should part ways. Because I've dealt with plenty of males underestimating me in the past, even one that supposedly loved me, and I won't put up with it again."

Fuck. Had she really said that?

Her dragon spoke up. *I think because he shared his past, and now you want to share yours.*

Quiet, dragon.

Antony's voice prevented her beast from replying. "I picked you to be my partner for this mission for a reason, Iris—I trust you to watch my back. So don't ever bloody think I underestimate you. You're talented and brilliant and amazing. Shall I go on?"

She turned toward him and blinked at how close his face was to hers. The fire flashing in his eyes said he meant it, too.

And the small crack around her heart doubled in size. "No. I-I believe you."

Time slowed as they stared at one another. For a second, she thought Antony might lean in and kiss her.

But then he cleared his throat and retreated. Before she could process her disappointment, he said, "If you think I'm not going to ask about the arsehole who under-estimated you in the past, the one who most definitely didn't deserve your love, then you don't know me at all."

She frowned. "I'd rather not talk about it."

He quirked an eyebrow. "I just shared the worst day of my life. Why won't you share a little with me, too, Iris? I think it'll help me understand you better. For working together on the mission, of course."

"But I thought we were on a schedule?"

"We are. But we'll just have to skip a stop at the service station for food and pick something up along the way. Which means we have time for this."

Part of her wanted to finally share the burden. One she'd never shared with anyone, not even Cooper and Brodie.

But another part of her knew that doing so would widen the crack in the wall around her heart, the wall she needed to protect herself.

Her dragon spoke up. *Just do it. He knows how to keep secrets and would never share it with the world.*

You have a lot of trust in him.

He's revealed some weak moments, things we could use against him, if we really wanted to. And yet, he trusts us. I like him.

Don't go getting ideas, dragon.

Her beast sniffed. *I'm done arguing. Eventually, you'll see it my way.*

I won't.

For now, just tell him. That way, we'll be even, and he won't have to worry about us using his past against him since he'll have something just as painful from us, aye?

Antony wouldn't cause us pain.

Aye, I know. I'm just glad you realize it, too.

Not wanting to think too hard on that, she searched Antony's brown eyes. Eyes that were both curious and yet almost...warm. As if begging her to trust him with this.

She finally said, "I will, as long as you don't interrupt me with constant demands for his name, or voicing threats. Whilst I appreciate the sentiment, it'll only make this take longer. And the less I have to talk about the bastard, the better."

"I promise. For now. But even if you don't tell me, I'll know his name soon enough. His punishment will depend on how much he hurt you."

She frowned. "There you go, sounding like a protective male dragon-shifter again."

"Don't try to distract me. Tell me what happened, Iris. Please."

It was the please that did it. After taking a deep breath, Iris reached back to memories she'd long ago buried. "It was during my time with the army. There was a human I met early on, one who trained me and I often sparred with. He was unlike any other human I'd met before—strong, intelligent, just as stubborn as me, and more accepting of dragon-shifters than I was used to. As soon as I finished my training and was no longer his student, we started spending a lot of time together.

"In the beginning, it was nice. He teased me, flirted, and made me feel special. I've always had trouble with males, especially dragon-shifter ones, because they never thought I could protect myself. And this male, well, he knew I could. However, once I started to perform better than him—with commendations and getting assigned more and more responsibilities—things began to change."

"And not for the better, I take it?" Antony asked.

Iris shook her head. "It started with little comments about there being easier standards for females. He said that if I was held to the same ones as males, I never would've advanced so far. And yet I *was* held to higher standards than the humans since I'm a dragon-shifter. And to even be admitted to the British Army for training, I had to pass the same tests as the male dragons from my clan. I worked hard, so bloody hard, and yet not having a dick meant I would never be good enough."

She clenched her fingers into a fist, remembering her ex's words: *If you were a man, you'd never have been given that last assignment. They just wanted good PR, showing off the most promising female dragon-shifter. Eventually, they'll move on and you'll be stuck, same as me.*

Antony's voice snapped her back to the present. "So it seems we both have things to prove. Even though your record shows how fucking brilliant you are, I can make sure you're credited in the press releases once we catch these bastards."

"No, I don't want fame and glory. That human male means nothing to me now."

After raising his hand, Antony lightly caressed her

cheek. Iris leaned into the warm, soft touch as he said, "Well, he was a fool. And one day soon, him and everyone who belittled you will realize it."

"Antony, don't do anything stupid."

"Oh, I'm far too experienced for that. I know how to make someone's life miserable with a single phone call."

She searched his gaze, and the mixture of determination, anger—for her, not at her—and something she couldn't define made her want to share more with him. This male seemed different from the others. In a good way.

Her dragon spoke up. *Of course he is. He tests males for bullshit right away, aye?*

Antony cupped her cheek, and despite her better judgment, she leaned more into his touch.

She nearly placed her hand over his when his phone rang. With a curse, he said, "Sorry, but I have to take that," before picking it up.

He didn't try to hide his conversation with her, albeit it was one-sided. Something about the press and news getting out.

After he told the person to take care of it, he hung up and grimaced. "The dragon hunters have uploaded videos and made posts about an upcoming dragon civil war, and it's catching fire."

"And, sadly, fact-checking means nothing anymore, aye?"

"Unfortunately, yes. However, I have some of the best PR people in the world on tap, and they're trying to mitigate the damage as best as they can. But the sooner we can find the rest of the rogue dragon-shifters and whoever is making this gas, the better. Humans like a villain to pin things on. So if we give them one, along with some strategic events or interviews with dragon-shifter leaders, it might stop the pitchforks." He turned on the engine. "Which means we need to hurry to the Peak District. I need to make several calls along the way, but just know that later, once we have a moment, I want to know you better, Iris Mahajan. Much better."

His cryptic words made her heart thump harder in her chest. Did he really want to woo her and kiss her and work on demolishing the wall around her heart?

Her dragon spoke up. *He'd better. Otherwise, I might have to try. He's not like other males.*

No, he's not. And yet, I'm still worried about this blowing up in my face, like the last time I let someone in.

That was over a decade ago, and we were young, aye? And Antony's isn't some young male, out to prove himself. He's done that already, has confidence, and realizes strength doesn't always mean using brute force.

Iris wasn't sure how to respond, especially since the more her dragon talked, the more she wanted to stop fighting her attraction and give Antony a chance.

Eventually, as Antony took call after call, she fell asleep to dreams of her laughing at something Antony said before taking him to bed and claiming him as her own.

Chapter Eleven

For the first time in a long time, Antony wished his job was a little less demanding. Between him sharing his past with Iris, her comforting him, and him learning about the arsehole who'd made her double-down to prove her abilities, he'd made a decision—to stop pretending he didn't want Iris Mahajan.

And he wanted more than a mere romp in the sheets. He wanted to let her shine, make sure everyone bloody well knew how good she was, and then take care of her at home. Make her laugh, make her moan his name, and maybe try to build a life with her.

It'd taken him hours of driving to finally accept he wanted all of that, of course. Because he still worried that his past would repeat and another woman he fancied would end up hurt.

Or dead.

Then he remembered not only was Iris highly

skilled, she could also shift into a dragon. While yes, she had weaknesses to certain drugs and weapons in that form, she had a lot more strengths in it, too.

Not that the dragonwoman had any idea about his plans for her. She slept most of the way, and he couldn't bring himself to wake her. Yes, because she needed the sleep. But also because it showed she trusted him. Maybe not completely, but it was a start.

When he finally turned onto the last single-track road leading to their destination, the car bumped along the uneven ground and Iris slowly woke up, rubbing her eyes as she asked, "Where are we?"

Ignoring how her sleep-tinged voice sent a rush of wanting through him—would she sound that way waking up in his bed too?—he replied, "Nearly to our destination."

"You still won't tell me more than that?"

"Whilst this car is heavily protected against any listening tech or devices, I want to wait until we're inside our destination, which is even more secure."

She glanced out the window. And while he could only see what the headlights highlighted, her keen dragon eyesight would see the sharp peaks and rugged beauty of the Peak District. On either side of the car were high, jagged hills. Ones that would hide them from almost everyone, including anyone flying overhead.

Within minutes, Antony turned into the secret entrance and waited in front of what looked like a solid rock surface. However, a pole appeared from the ground, until he could allow it to scan his retinas. Then the rock surface slid to the side, creating a space big enough for him to drive his car through.

Once he pulled his car to the side and turned off the engine, he said, "Follow me. We're nearly there, and I promise to fill you in."

She nodded, and they both exited the car. The space looked like a sealed-in cave, but he went to a section on the far east side and placed his hand against the stone. It moved aside, and he had to both scan his palm and his retina again. Then he said, "Code Bravo-Oscar-November-Delta Eight-Niner."

Iris raised her eyebrows. "Really?"

He shrugged. "One of the techs rotates the phrases, not me."

Because in the phonetic alphabet used by armies and broadcasters, it spelled out Bond 89. The tech staff always teased Antony about being an old, retired Bond in his eighties instead of his forties.

A door slid open, and he motioned for Iris to follow. As soon as the door closed behind them, another appeared, leading into a long corridor full of doors. "Now, we can talk. Come on. I have an office here, and I promise to tell you everything."

"Is this the part where you say you will, but I can never leave or you'll have to kill me?"

He snorted. "Nothing so dramatic, my dear. You want the same thing as me—to end the dragon hunters.

And that means you wouldn't do anything to jeopardize that goal."

"So practical. No doubt, that irritates some."

"Not so many. Remember, I weed out the insecure ones early."

He approached his office and entered the outer room where his executive assistant sat at the desk.

Eddie rolled his wheelchair from behind the desk to hand Antony a folder. "The latest."

"Thank you." He gestured from Iris to his assistant and back again. "Iris, this is Eddie. He was my bloody best reconnaissance person until he lost his legs. Eddie, this is Iris, my partner for this mission."

Iris shook the human male's hand. "Nice to meet you. I hope the other side fared worse."

Eddie grinned. "Took them all out, I did. I would tell you more, but I'm not allowed."

Antony rolled his eyes. "Eventually, you can tell Iris your story. No need to guilt-trip me in front of our guest."

"Hey, I take what I can get."

"Right, I need to go over some things with Iris, as well as analyze these reports. Don't disturb me unless it's a top-level priority issue."

"A bomb could go off in your office, and I would stay at my post."

Iris blinked, and Antony explained, "There are some strange protocols here. I'll explain. Come on."

After nodding his thanks to Eddie, he used another

retinal scanner before entering his office. It was more like a small flat with a mini-kitchen, sofa bed, desk, and bathroom off to the side.

He immediately went to the kitchen, filled the kettle, and switched it on. Once he turned to face Iris, he said, "As soon as the tea is ready, we'll get down to business."

She snorted. "So British."

"I can't really drink alcohol in my line of work, so I take what I can get. Which means lots of tea and eating far too many biscuits."

As her eyes slowly traveled down his body, his cock stirred. She said, "You can't even tell."

Clearing his throat, he turned to retrieve mugs and tea bags. "I still train and also enjoy biking when I get the chance. There's something about the wind in your hair as you pedal through the countryside, far from the city and work and the constant barrage of technology, that soothes your soul."

The kettle clicked off, he poured, and turned to face Iris. She tilted her head and said, "The longer I'm around you, the less I understand you. Here you have the best technological gadgets in the world, and yet you long to ride a bicycle far away from it all."

"What, you don't have any hobbies unrelated to your work?"

"I like to read, but most of the time I'm training or working."

"Because you have to, or because you never feel as if you're good enough?"

Turning away from him, she headed for the small table and sat down. "Enough about me. I want to know about this place, what it's used for, and why we're here."

He sighed, knowing when to pick his battles. "Fine." After retrieving some biscuits from the cupboard, he carried everything over to the table and sat down. "This is the central hub of dragon-related matters in the UK, my dear. The place near London is mainly for research. Well, and keeping track of Skyhunter."

"And what does that mean, exactly? And why have I never heard about it before?"

Pushing the biscuits toward her, he answered, "This is going to take a while, so have some sugar."

Only once she sipped her tea and nibbled on a biscuit did Antony lean forward and prop his elbows on the table. He took a few more seconds to prepare himself because Iris might want to punch him or cry off or who knew what once she learned about the past and what they'd done from this place.

Iris was this close to growling and telling Antony to hurry the hell up. She could be patient most of the time, but this male had a flair for the dramatic.

However, since he'd probably just argue and get even more off track, she ate part of a biscuit and drank some tea. Antony nodded and finally spoke again. "About five years before the sacrifice program began with the dragon-shifters, both the Department of Dragon Affairs and MI5 decided they needed to monitor the dragons in this country closely. Since distrust of dragon-shifters was still high back then, some were afraid the human sacrifices would be bullied into saying one thing whilst in reality experiencing another."

Iris frowned. "And yet, they still allowed the females to live with the dragon clans to try to conceive a child."

"Yes, I know—in retrospect, it's a bit callous. But the National Health Service and the government were desperate to get some dragon's blood to help with the HIV and AIDS epidemic in the 1980s, so they thought it was worth the risk."

She was about to interject again when Antony beat her to it. "I don't agree with most of what they did back then, or with their way of thinking. I'm just trying to let you know where you are and how it came to be. If you keep interrupting, this will take all night. And I rather need a nap after driving for so long."

For a split second, guilt rushed through her. Iris had slept most of the drive, and Antony had been awake for who knew how long. "Aye, I understand. You may continue."

His lips twitched. "As you wish, my dear. So back to the 1980s—they wanted to keep tabs on everyone. Stonefire was the most open to taking sacrifices, and so they built this facility inside some of the rocky hills in the Peak District because it was close enough without being too close. They also created smaller, equally camouflaged, watch posts closer to Stonefire itself. And before you ask, the smaller ones were shut down over a decade ago."

"But before they were, the people working for this place were essentially spying on dragon-shifters, aye?"

"Yes. Eventually, a Stonefire Protector discovered one of the observation stations. Knowing what to look for, they easily found another, and another. Soon the clan leader at the time demanded a meeting, and a formal agreement was signed, ending most of the spying."

"Most, but not all?"

"We still monitor flight patterns, both in case we have to investigate accidents and to see if a human complaint is valid. Most of that is done via CCTV these days, though. Video evidence is more powerful than someone's word or log in a book."

"And Lochguard?"

"There are cameras and a few staff monitoring the air there, too. Usually, an injured person from my team gets relocated to the Highlands since there's less air traffic, making it less stressful. However, posts up there have become more important in recent years since they've monitored the rogue dragon-shifters living in the Cairngorms. And before you ask, we've reviewed the footage we have from the day of the mass murders. However, someone knew what they were doing and avoided the cameras. Because of that, I think there may be a leak inside the greater Wicked Security team."

"Hence the dragon clan and security team pairings, as well as the reason for keeping individual assignments secret."

"Yes, my dear. I saved the best lead we have to finding the culprit for us." He tilted his head. "But I need to know—are you okay working in a former dragon spying facility?"

"It's strange to think about how humans were so worried back then. Aye, I know there are plenty of humans who still hate us. But creating a secret hideout to spy on us is a wee bit extreme."

"To be fair, a dragon-shifter in their dragon form can be pretty bloody scary when you're merely a human. All of those pointy teeth and claws, you know. Not to mention the fact you could just step on a human and that's it, they're dead."

She raised an eyebrow. "And yet, I've never seen you afraid of us."

"Ah, but I've been working with dragon-shifters for over twenty years now, and they've saved my life more than once. I know better than to fall for rumors or propaganda. But not everyone has my experience or perspective."

"And that is something we need to fix later, aye? Once the dragon hunters are finally defeated."

Antony nodded. "The DDA Director is determined to make things more equal for dragon-shifters, no matter what. And she's a powerful ally to have." He tilted his head. "So you have no problem working with me and my team, even though our origins began as mistrustful, bigoted humans who wanted to know your every secret?"

Iris shrugged. "I don't have to like what was done here, especially considering all the restrictions humans put on us for so long. However, defeating the dragon hunters and stopping a genocidal bio-weapon attack on my kind is more important. I'm more worried about the potential leak and traitor from your department working with one of my fellow Protectors."

"I know for certain that Trina and Joseph are loyal and would never betray me. I'm mostly confident the other three I sent with the Protectors are as well. The intel I've gathered points more to a formerly injured recruit who is probably resentful of being assigned desk work."

She raised her brows. "Like Eddie, your assistant?"

"As much as I wouldn't like it, it's possible. I try to keep some of the suspects close. And most of them work here, not in London. The last thing I need is Dr. Turner's research and discoveries getting out."

"So that means you still can't share everything with me?"

He sighed. "Almost. There are a few things that if I revealed, I would be relocated and never heard from again. I'm working on higher clearance for you, but it takes time."

She blinked. "You want to give me higher clearance?"

"I trust you, Iris. And you were right earlier—going into a situation blind can get people hurt. Your clearance should come through in a few days. In the meantime, there's a former rogue dragon-shifter who left the group to go live on her own. One I've convinced to let us visit and chat with. After hearing how half the rogue dragons were murdered, she's afraid she could also be a target."

Antony yawned, and Iris said, "I hope it's in the morning, aye? Because if you try to do anything half-asleep, you'll fuck up."

He chuckled. "Never one to mince words, are you?"

"No. I'd rather not see you die."

"Growing fond of me, are you?"

She rolled her eyes. "Only you would make that into a kind of flirtation. But no, I don't want you to die. I want more answers, and to finally end the threats to my clan. You're key to that."

He stood and moved to her side of the table. "Is that the only reason?"

Iris locked eyes with the human, and she saw a flash of yearning. Despite all his bluster and teasing and confidence, he was unsure about her.

Her dragon spoke up. *He's showing yet another vulnerability with us. Answer him truthfully.*

Iris murmured, "No, it's not the only reason."

Triumph surged in his gaze before vanishing, replaced with a smile that reached his eyes. He put out a hand. "Then I'd better do as you ask. Let me show you to your quarters, and we'll both get some sleep."

Her dragon said, *Maybe we should just share quarters. That would be better.*

Ignoring her beast, Iris placed her hand in his, and Antony gently pulled her upward. She now stood only a few inches from him, and she swore she could feel the heat radiating from his body.

He wasn't much taller than her, either, which put their faces close together as well. Not for the first time, she wondered how such a handsome male was still alone. Or, at least, she thought he was.

Before she could think better of it, she blurted, "You're not seeing or sleeping with anyone else, are you?"

"No." He gently brushed some hair behind her ear. "Everyone else is lacking compared to you."

It was corny and ridiculous, and yet Iris couldn't help smiling. "Good. Because I don't share."

"Neither do I."

Tension hummed between them. It would be easy, so easy, to lean over and kiss him.

But that could start a mate-claim frenzy, and Iris wasn't ready for it. She wasn't completely against the idea of finding her true mate, but until she could tame some of the dangers, she wouldn't risk it.

Which meant resisting the human's tempting lips and stepping back a few feet. He frowned, but she spoke before he could. "You need to rest, Antony. We both do. The sooner we take care of the threats, the sooner we can think of..."

"Of what, my dear?"

"Of other things."

He smiled again as he shook his head. "So circumspect. Let me be a bit more forthright." He leaned forward and whispered, "The sooner we take care of the threats, the sooner you can think of me making you moan, having you pull my hair, and you telling me exactly how to please you."

Her cheeks heated. "Antony."

He raised an eyebrow. "What? I'm just being truthful. And it's a type of motivation, right?"

"Maybe."

Antony reached out, took her hand, and kissed the back of it. The light touch sent a rush of heat through her body, straight between her legs.

He murmured, "You're the very best type of motivation for me, Iris, and more than worth the wait."

As she tried to think of how to reply to that—Iris had little experience with males and flirting and wooing—the human dropped her hand and moved to the door of his office. "Come on, let's head into a more public space. Because if you keep looking at me like that, as if you want to devour me, I might say to hell with any sleep and that wouldn't be good for the mission."

"Aye, the mission."

Her dragon huffed. *We can do both.*

Not now, dragon. But maybe later.

Hmm. At least you're coming around, aye?

Realizing that she was standing and saying nothing,

she pointed to her eyes. "Whilst I understand the benefit of wearing these special contacts in the city or in large groups of humans, they probably make me look like a dolt when I don't reply right away."

"Dolt, huh?" She narrowed her eyes, and he chuckled. "Fine, fine. I'm not one to criticize, given how I usually talk like a posh twit. Mostly on purpose, since it unnerves people."

She joined him at the door. "You seem to be rather good at unnerving people in general, aye?"

"It's a skill, I assure you." He pressed a button, and the door slid open. "Now, come on. We'll stop by the small cafe on the way to your quarters so you can have something to eat. You were sleeping on the road, and I didn't want to wake you."

Her stomach rumbled at that exact moment, the traitor. "Aye, that sounds good." She noticed the assistant was gone. "Where did he go?"

"Eddie's shift ended soon after we went into my office." He offered his arm, like in the days of old.

Iris hesitantly threaded hers through his, instantly recognizing how firm his muscles were. She squeezed his arm with hers. "Definitely fit."

Had she really just said that out loud?

Her dragon merely laughed inside her head.

Antony gently tugged, and they started walking. "This way, before you make me change my mind about needing sleep."

And as he pointed out the various rooms along the

way, she mentally sighed in relief. His charm was dangerous, and it wouldn't take much more for her to forget her purpose here and proceed to strip him, ride him, and see if he really lived up to his words.

Her dragon spoke up. *Aye, we'll do that soon enough. First the enemies, then we claim our male.*

Iris should argue that he wasn't theirs. But she was tired, ignored her beast, and did her best not to think about what life would be like in the future if Antony Holbrook was indeed hers to claim.

Chapter Twelve

The next morning, Iris eyed the car and sighed. "I hate these things."

Antony raised an eyebrow. "Unfortunately, it's illegal for me to hitch a basket to you and fly through the air. If you'd even allow it. So this is all we have."

She slid into the car, and once he did too, she replied, "I wouldn't mind carrying you, and I even know how to keep you from falling out since we train with rock-filled baskets. Because in emergencies, aye, we're allowed to carry humans in the air."

"I highly doubt your dislike of cars would count as an emergency. Plus, we couldn't remain inconspicuous, given where we're going, and we need to be."

He turned on the engine and backed up as she said, "It's going to take forever to reach Inverness with a car, though."

Antony had barely told her the basics of their assignment today—they needed to investigate a lead in Inverness, Scotland—before herding them out the door and to the car.

Her dragon spoke up. *At least he is sharing information, aye?*

I know, I know. Now, hush.

Once Antony drove out of the facility and back to the single-track road, she asked, "If it was so important to drive here in the dark, why are we now driving in the daylight?"

Antony pressed a button on the dashboard before replying, "There. My latest gadget should keep prying ears from hearing anything said in here. To answer your question, I'm more careful about leaving the research facility in London than leaving this place in the Peak District. It's fairly common knowledge, if you know where to look, that Wicked Security is set up here. As such, we're prepared for any and all attacks. However, the research facility in London is harder to protect, since it's not as isolated. The less back-and-forth traffic we show, the better."

She suspected there was more he wasn't telling her. However, Iris knew her special clearance hadn't come through yet, so she didn't push and focused on what she could ask. "Aye, well, then back to Inverness. You promised that once we were on the road, you'd tell me more about what we need to do there."

He nodded. "We're going to visit my former protégé,

Jude Nickerson. At one point, I'd picked him to replace me when I retired. However, after he had a run-in with a fringe group of former Dragon Knights and broke his back, he couldn't move like he used to, not even after he was fully recovered from surgery. In fact, he had to be retired from the field altogether."

"Which also means he isn't your replacement any longer, aye?"

"No, unfortunately not. Whoever has this position needs to work long hours, move around a lot, and be able to dash away, when the need arises. Even if Jude is bloody brilliant at intelligence gathering and strategy, my superior made the call about stationing him in Inverness, to watch the skies instead."

Iris tried to imagine being queued up to head an entire secret spy agency and then having it ripped away. It would be devastating. "Surely he knows it wasn't your decision, right?"

"Yes, but he's still resentful and thinks I didn't fight hard enough for him. Part of me thinks he wants to be put back out to die in action. The other part of me thinks he's still struggling to accept the drastic changes to his life. Either way, I received some intelligence two days ago, which makes me think he's the leak and that he's changed sides to help the dragon hunters."

Antony explained how one of his team discovered Jude's online username for a secret forum, one most people could never find, and had learned of his vitriol about the British government, and especially the Department of Dragon Affairs. He believed they ruined his life on purpose by not taking care of the Dragon Knights sooner.

Further digging had revealed Jude offering information to the right buyer. While Antony's team was still trying to confirm if Jude had sold anything, it was definitely worth a look.

When Antony finished, Iris studied his profile. "It must feel as if he's betrayed you, aye? Even if he doesn't end up being the leak."

Antony's lips firmed a few beats before he said, "I'm more disappointed. Most of us suffer tragedy and set back at one time or another, especially in this line of work. And whilst I understand the frustration of not being able to walk very long and often relying on a cane considering he could run marathons before the incident, betraying us, me, and the country is extreme. I keep thinking I missed something when I first recruited him."

Iris laid a hand on Antony's shoulder and squeezed. "As much as you don't want to admit it, you're not perfect, Antony Holbrook. No one is. And sometimes, you'll be wrong, aye?"

He sighed dramatically. "I suppose."

She poked his side, and he chuckled as she said, "Be serious and don't deflect. Do you really blame yourself for Jude's actions?"

"Sometimes. And yes, I know that's irrational. It's not as if I put a mind-control chip in his brain and can control him like in a video game."

"Wait, do you have mind-control chips?"

His lips twitched. "That's classified."

"Ugh, you're awful, aye? Teasing me like that."

He winked. "Once your clearance comes through, ask me again. I'll just have to find something else to tease you about."

"As long as you don't start practicing any stand-up routines, that's fine."

"Well, you *are* trapped in this car with me for hours. Maybe I should try a few. I'm a bit rusty, but I bet I can make you laugh."

"Whilst I'm tempted to see you try, I'd rather you tell me more about the operations in Inverness, Jude, and anything else that could help us once we get there."

"You're overly focused, but I like it. Makes me wonder what you'll be like, with such focus, when naked."

Her dragon tried to flash images of Antony's cock in their mouth, but she pushed it aside. *Stop it, or I'll put you in a mental maze.*

You're no fun.

Save your fantasies for later. Maybe you can try some of them, aye?

You'd better keep your word.

I didn't give my word.

I'm going to pretend you did.

She growled out loud, and Antony said, "Now I want to know what your dragon said to you."

"It's rude to ask a dragon-shifter that, aye?"

"Perhaps. But I'd like to think we're past the façade of formality, given how I promised to eventually make you scream with my mouth."

Her dragon laughed. *Between him and me, you don't stand a chance.*

Ignoring her beast, she replied to Antony. "If I told you what she said, you'd probably crash the car."

"Tsk, tsk, I can concentrate through almost anything, my dear. Now I have to know."

She muttered, "I don't know who's worse—you or her."

"Hmm, why do you say that?"

Looking at him, she frowned. "You're human. You shouldn't have heard that."

"I may be older than you, but I'm not deaf."

She eyed his ears. "You have special hearing devices for when you work with dragon-shifters, don't you? Ones that won't short out."

"It's something we're working on. But no, I just have keen hearing. So keep that in mind for future mutterings. Aye?"

"Are you mocking me?"

He laughed. "No. But it's getting easier and easier to figure out how to rile you up, my dear. It's fun."

Her inner beast spoke up. *Tell him things I say and flash into your mind, and that might rile him.*

As her dragon continued showing some of her sex fantasies, Iris smiled and said, "I could unsettle you."

"Can you, now? I'm intrigued."

She leaned over and whispered, "My dragon has some rather interesting fantasies, aye?"

"Let's see if you can shock me or not, then."

Her dragon laughed. *This is going to be fun.*

For once, I agree with you.

Then stop stalling.

"Well, let's start with one of the tamer ones, aye? With me in control, she wants to blindfold you, tease you with a feather and my tongue before taking your cock into my mouth. Then I'd tease you, oh-so-slowly, with licks and light nibbles, until you get close. But then I'd back away and tease another part of you until you beg. Then I'd suck your dick again, pull away, and repeat until you're sweating and all but begging."

His voice was a little husky as he said, "I don't beg in the bedroom, Iris."

"That sounds like a challenge, aye?"

"One I'm going to meet, tit-for-tat, so keep that in mind, my dear."

"You say that as if it's a bad thing."

He groaned, and Iris grinned. Her dragon said, *I told you, he's easy to discombobulate with the right approach.*

Well, he is male, after all.

Antony said, "Iris—" but then the mobile phone Antony had given her—a secure one her clan could contact her with—vibrated.

Mentally cursing the interruption, she hit Answer, and Finn Stewart's voice came over the line. "Iris, Zoe is missing."

Her stomach dropped. "What?"

"She went to meet with the DDA liaison in Inverness yesterday evening but didn't return. Cooper thought she might've stayed the night somewhere since it's a long drive. However, no one has seen or heard from her since her check-in right before her meeting."

And since Zoe checked in with her brother every day when away from the clan, to placate his worries, the silence was unusual. Alarm bells rang inside her head. "Tell me everything you know."

"You're with Antony Holbrook, aye? Put me on speakerphone." She did as asked and Finn continued, "One of our Protectors, Zoe Watson, went to meet with the DDA liaison in Inverness yesterday and hasn't been heard from since. Worse than that, no one can locate the liaison himself."

Antony stated, "And the liaison was Jude Nickerson."

Finn said, "Aye, and judging by the tone of your voice, there's something you're not telling me."

Iris shared a glance with Antony and raised her eyebrows. How much could they share?

Antony took the lead. "Let's just say we were on our way to meet him. We'll be in Inverness later today and will investigate Zoe's disappearance. For now, just tell us everything you know about your Protector's last whereabouts and any other pertinent information."

Once Finn had rattled off the details and said goodbye, Iris asked, "If Jude kidnapped Zoe, then why? They could've taken any of the rogue dragon-shifters they murdered instead, for whatever reason."

"One thing I didn't share about the mass dragon grave is that it only contained males and females past childbearing age."

For a second, she tried to think of why that would be, beyond female dragons only being slightly weaker and smaller than their male counterparts. It couldn't be for breeding reasons since the gene to shift into a dragon was dominant and always passed to the offspring, no matter which parent gave it to them.

And then she remembered something about Dr. Sid's research. "Female dragon-shifters paired with human males tend to have more female offspring. And Dr. Sid Jackson on Stonefire recently discovered that female dragon's blood is slightly more potent than a male's."

Antony nodded. "Yes, I saw the reports. Both have healing properties but female dragon's blood makes a human heal faster. Some even think it might make the original human stronger going forward, with minute genetic shifts."

"But wouldn't that have been something the DDA or even the clans would've figured out sooner?"

He shrugged one shoulder. "Maybe, maybe not. Because of how strict the laws were until recently, mainly forbidding female dragons from mating human males, the dragon-shifter population skewed heavily male. As such, the blood given in exchange for a sacrifice has primarily been from males."

She rubbed her forehead. "I never thought being a Protector meant having to think about biology and genetics."

"I wish I could say everything just comes to me, but alas, no. Dr. Turner gives me bi-weekly briefings on the latest dragon-shifter research. It's not exactly a hobby of mine, but rather something I have to know, given how much the dragon hunters are interested in dragon's blood." He tapped his phone's screen and brought up a list of coded contacts. "I need to make some calls. So, sadly, my comedy routines will have to wait."

"I can't believe I'm saying this, but I'd rather hear your jokes any day than have one of my coworkers in danger."

"I know. And I'm going to do all that I can to find and save her, I promise."

She glanced over at him. "Aye, I know."

He gently patted her leg. "Now, let's see what I can find out. I'll have all the calls on speaker, and if you have a question, go ahead and ask it."

"But I don't have my special clearance yet."

"Temporarily, for this issue, you have it. My boss can take it up with me later."

Before she could thank Antony, he started calling people. And Iris settled down, eager to find out what she could about Zoe, Jude, and if her disappearance was connected to the murdered rogue dragons or the dragon hunters.

Chapter Thirteen

"**Z**oe, Zoe, wake up."

Zoe Watson tried to ignore the voice, hoping she could just go back to sleep. But then someone shook her, and her eyes shot open.

While she vaguely noticed the bars and stone walls that denoted an old jail cell, it was the person sitting next to her that garnered her full attention—her cousin, Rebecca Watson.

The cousin who'd gone off with her parents to join the rogue, clanless dragon-shifters.

But how was she here? Why?

Even though her brain was a little foggy, Zoe glanced around and noticed another female dragon-shifter in the same cell, and then more across the way.

And even if she didn't remember everyone's names, she never forgot a face. They were all in the file of UK clan traitors, the ones everyone thought had gone to live

144

with the clanless dragon-shifters in Cairngorms National Park.

Even if she didn't know where she was or how she'd gotten there, she had to tread carefully. Rebecca might be her cousin, but she'd disowned Zoe and her family the day she'd left Lochguard.

Slowly, she tried to stand, but her body was heavy, and she could barely lift her head.

Rebecca said, "No, don't try to get up. You'll be weak for a wee while yet."

Doing her best to sit up and lean against the wall, she tried reaching out to her dragon.

Silence.

Fuck. She only hoped it wasn't permanent.

Focus, Zoe. Rely on your training and don't give anything away. She studied her cousin's shorter form. Her skin was a lighter brown than she remembered, and her reddish-brown hair was shorn close to her head. She'd also lost some weight.

Deciding now would be a good time to get information—she needed to keep focused on anything but the fact she was now a prisoner and work would do that—she asked, "How long have you been here?"

Rebecca shrugged. "I don't know. There aren't any windows, and no one tells us anything."

The other female dragon-shifter in the room spoke up. "It's been over a week, at least judging by my leg hair."

Her accent was Welsh. She was older than Zoe, with

dark hair that had a sprinkling of gray and blue eyes. She tried to recall the name, but couldn't. So she asked, "Who are you?"

The Welsh female raised a dark eyebrow. "A bit demanding, aren't you?"

Zoe didn't blink an eye at the female's tone. "I don't know how much my cousin shared whilst I was unconscious, but I'm a Protector."

And I'm the best chance we have at escaping, she left unsaid. For all Zoe knew, the place was bugged.

The Welsh female tilted her head. "That just means you're happy we're stuck in here so you can interrogate us, right? Since we're the enemy?"

Another female voice from the cell across the way said in a Northern English accent, "At least listen to what she has to say, Bethan. She might have ideas to help us."

Bethan glared at the other female. "Thanks for sharing my name. Let me return the favor, Chelsea."

Chelsea rolled her eyes. "She might already know our names. I'm sure they keep a list of us all."

Zoe decided a wee bit of honesty might help her get more information. "I know all of your faces, but not your names. My cousin, aye, I know her. And anyone from Lochguard, like Rosie in the cell with you over there. But not the rest."

Chelsea studied her a second before replying, "My mate was a Protector. I listened and learned a few things." She glanced down the row of cells. "But I don't know where they put him."

Bloody hell, they didn't know.

Zoe debated telling them. But false hope was cruel, even to clan traitors, and it might give her more of an in with these females. "I don't know for certain who, but half of the rogue dragon-shifters are dead. We found them in a mass grave near your settlement."

Rebecca asked, "How do we know you're telling the truth and not just playing on our sympathies?"

She met her cousin's gaze. "Believe me, or don't, aye? But I've seen some of the autopsy pictures, as well as video footage of the mass grave. Someone killed most of the male dragon-shifters living in Cairngorms, and it wasn't me or any of the main clans who did it." She nearly reached out to her cousin, but held back. "Your father was one of the dead, Rebecca. I'm so sorry."

Her cousin shook her head vehemently. "No, you're lying. Dad was one of the strongest. He can't be dead. He just can't."

The main reason Rebecca had left Lochguard was to follow her parents. She was barely twenty, still young, and Rebecca hadn't held the same hatred for humans as her mother and especially her father.

Still, Zoe didn't know if Rebecca had been brainwashed or conditioned to hate humans even more since the last time they'd talked. Which meant she couldn't let her guard down. "Despite everything, I wish I were. I remember Christmases with our families together, when we were kids. I never wanted my uncle to be murdered, no matter our differences."

Rebecca paced the room, clenching and unclenching her fingers. "I don't believe you. For all we know, the regular clans are behind this, all of this, and they put you in here to get us on your side. To tug at our connection and somehow make me forget that your mother is human."

And there it was—the reason Zoe never understood how her uncle, who was her father's brother, could've grown to hate humans so much. He'd seemed fine around Zoe's mother while she was still alive. It was only long after her death that he hadn't been.

She leaned more heavily against the wall, hating how weak and tired she was. However, during her Protector training, she'd learned how to push on a wee bit longer, when necessary. And she needed to know more. Much more.

So she did her best to keep her voice strong as she said, "Aye, my mother was human, and I loved her. That is something I can never change. But I would never kill anyone because they felt uncomfortable around her, or around me. Bloody hell, if I did that anytime I go into a village, when they stare at me as if I'm some sort of unicorn because of my skin color, I would've been a serial killer by now." She leaned forward a little. "I vow that Lochguard, or any of the UK clans, had nothing to do with what happened to you or the males in the mass grave."

Even though vows were extremely important to dragon-shifters, it might not be enough. So Zoe also willed the truth to shine from her eyes.

Eventually, Rebecca turned away from her and said quietly, "If I find out that you're bloody toying with me, Zoe, I don't care if we're related, I'll make you pay. Maybe hand you over to the dragon hunters myself, once we get out of here."

Did that mean it was someone besides the dragon hunters who had captured them?

Zoe wanted to push, to see if there was some sort of connection between the rogue dragon-shifters and the dragon hunters. However, Bethan's voice beat her to it. "She might believe you, but I'm still skeptical. How did they die? Who is behind it all, if not your clan members? Where are we, even?"

As she'd been talking, Zoe had casually scanned the surrounding cells without being obvious. And everyone was female. And still in childbearing age.

Back at Lochguard, Cooper and the other Protectors had discussed why only males and older females had been in the mass grave. At least now she knew where the younger females had gone.

She wished she could reach out to her clan and see if they'd found out anything else. Her last update had been before she'd left Lochguard to meet with the DDA liaison in Inverness.

Inverness. She'd made it to the city, had gone to meet

the DDA liaison, and then nothing. Had the liaison drugged her? Why?

Aware everyone was staring at her, she decided to work on getting her memories back later. "I can tell you we didn't murder anyone until my dying breath, and you still wouldn't believe me. So let me ask you something else—who looks after you in here? Anyone you knew from before?"

Silence.

Zoe resisted a sigh. "Aye, well, then I'm not going to share any more information if you won't do the same. I'll remember this later, when we get rescued."

Bethan snorted. "Who would rescue us? They might come for you, maybe. But I doubt Rhydian would care if I lived or died, now that he's mated to that human of his."

Rhydian Griffiths was the leader of Clan Snowridge in Wales, and his mate was a human named Delaney. The Welsh leader had banished some clan members after they'd tried to hurt his female.

Zoe replied to the former Snowridge female, "What do you have against humans, I wonder?"

Bethan said, "Maybe everything is full of fairy stories about humans and dragons getting along in Scotland. However, the humans in Northern Wales have never wanted us there. And not even your celebrity human's book helped change that mindset."

No doubt she was referring to Melanie Hall-MacLeod's book about dragon-shifters, one that had changed the minds of a lot of humans when it came to dragons and their fears.

Chelsea, the female dragon across the way, growled. "That book just gave them more ammunition to use against us. Bram has a human mate, too. One who worked for the DDA, the agency that has kept us as second-class citizens. I despise her, and he'd probably rather see me in that supposed mass grave you found than ever try to help me."

Even though it would probably be fruitless, Zoe had to try. "Evie, Bram's mate, has helped us many times over. And the current DDA Director has been working with us more and more, trying to influence politicians to grant us more freedom."

Chelsea sneered. "Right, more freedom, but not true freedom. It should be us who rule over them. But no, the gutless leaders have continued to bend the knee toward the weak humans instead."

A new female dragon in Chelsea's cell spoke up, her accent making her from the south of England and probably from Clan Skyhunter. "Having a so-called strong leader who believes in dragon-shifter superiority isn't the solution. Marcus King was that way, at least before I left. Eventually, he became corrupt and worked with the humans. But he wasn't always that way, and instead took joy in punishing his own people."

Zoe zeroed in on the Skyhunter female. "Why didn't you go back, once Honoria and Asher took over?"

The pair were Skyhunter's new leaders and had been working on healing their clan after Marcus's reign.

The female hugged her arms around her body. "I don't want to get into it."

Chelsea shook her head. "Marcus King was greedy and not a true believer. I'd make a better leader, one who'd never give up trying to conquer the UK and then the rest of Europe."

Zoe replied, "Right, because you'd win against their anti-aircraft and anti-dragon artillery? I was in the military, remember? Dragon-shifters wouldn't stand a chance. Maybe before World War I, but not after."

Chelsea stood tall. "A great cause requires some sacrifice."

"Aye, well, then let's play along—what would you do once you supposedly conquered the UK, after all those casualties? You sound like a purist, which means you'd never let someone like me, of mixed human and dragon blood, to have any children. Will you put all the pure-blood females into breeding camps and make them pump out bairns until they die of exhaustion or complications?"

A few more of the females moved to the bars of their cells, clearly paying attention now.

If she could push Chelsea a little more—and have her go too far—it might give them all a shared enemy. While a long shot, it might make them trust Zoe a wee bit more. Maybe enough to answer simple questions about who took care of them and anyone who worked in this facility.

Chelsea glanced around, the area eerily silent, as everyone waited for her answer. She finally said, "I would never imprison anyone who shared my vision. But surely there must be others who wish to expand pure bloodlines. Even if we have to recruit other dragon-shifters from Europe or Africa, we can make it work."

Bethan raised an eyebrow. "Most of us have a human somewhere up in our family tree. So, what? Will you sterilize all of us that do? For something we can't control?"

Zoe wanted to point out the hypocrisy—the female wanted forgiveness for having human blood and yet hated all humans, which were the key to her existence—but it was getting harder and harder to keep her eyes open. The verbal sparring had taken its toll, given how she was still fighting the aftereffects of being drugged. So she merely listened.

Chelsea said, "We'll do our best to dilute the human blood as much as possible. It might mean forgetting about true mates or love to accomplish it, so pureblooded dragons are mated to those of mixed ancestry, but it'll be worth it in the end."

Some of them are truly lost, she thought to herself.

And as the females started to grumble and argue, Zoe's exhaustion weighed heavier and heavier until her eyes closed and the world went black.

Chapter Fourteen

By the time they reached Inverness, Antony had mostly gotten his anger under control.

Of all the bloody people who could've betrayed him, Jude would've been the last person on his list. He'd been so certain the man was trustworthy, and even with his souring mood after being moved to a desk job, Antony never would've suspected he would turn traitor.

And yet, by all accounts, he had.

The man was gone, had vanished without a trace, and techs at the Inverness DDA office were still assessing how much Jude had downloaded from the restricted servers.

Things were bad, really bad. And after all the praise and recommendations to promote Jude, Antony felt partially responsible, and knew he had to find the man as soon as possible.

As he and Iris walked into the nondescript house his team used occasionally in the city, he put up a hand, signaling Iris to wait, and went inside to do a check. After ensuring no one had entered since his last visit and that the place was free of any bugs or tampered equipment, he motioned for Iris to enter. Only once she locked the door did he say, "We need to change, quickly, or we'll be late for our meeting."

She raised a dark eyebrow. "Can you finally tell me who it's with?"

"An informant. One embedded deep inside the dragon hunters in Scotland. However, because he's so involved, he rarely meets with anyone from my team. But after finding so many dead dragon-shifters, it's worth the risk to see him."

"Are you sure it's wise to have me tag along? If he's seen with a dragon-shifter, they'll probably question, or even torture and kill, him."

"You won't be anywhere near me, so it should be fine. And I need you in my ear, in case there's a question I haven't thought of. I know a lot about dragon affairs in the UK, but not as much as you." He nodded toward the bag on the sofa. "Those should make you look like any other human in town. Inside are the special earpiece, as well as the microphone to place on the top of your back tooth. Now, hurry. We only have about ten minutes before we have to leave."

Iris rolled her eyes. "I'm not the type to take two hours to get ready."

She grabbed the bag, and Antony headed into the bedroom.

Iris had been brilliant and indispensable on the drive up to Inverness. She didn't interject during a call unless it was necessary, and always had a good point to bring up. He wished she could teach that skill to a few other people he knew.

And when the calls had ended and Antony had needed some silence to ponder and gather his thoughts, it hadn't felt strange or awkward. No, it'd been...nice. Comfortable. Almost as if they'd known each other forever.

The more time he spent with Iris, the more he wanted to finish this blasted mission to know her better. Woo her, kiss her, and show her other ways they fit together outside of work.

Push it aside for now and use it as a type of motivation.

Once he finished dressing and attaching his unde-tectable gadgets—including the soccer scarf to pretend he was supporting a team playing tonight—he walked into the living room and did a double-take.

When he'd asked one of his staff to get Iris some clothes for a regular Saturday night out, he'd expected jeans and a sweater.

However, Iris wore a dark blue dress that hugged across her breasts, to her trim waist, and down her long legs. The deep color made her skin glow. And since her hair was in a messy bun atop her head, he wanted nothing more than to nuzzle her neck and see if she smelled as good as she looked.

Iris crossed her arms over her chest. "Whoever picked this outfit must never work in the field. It's so impractical."

He smiled. "Yes, I agree. But there's nothing else here. Besides, think of it this way—it's a better form of camouflage. Anyone who knows you would never look twice at a beautiful woman in a dress, right?"

"You don't have to lay it on thick. But I'm warning you—if I need to pursue someone, I won't hesitate to rip the skirt off, aye?"

He walked over, took her hand, and kissed the back of it. Only once she met his gaze did he murmur, "You *are* beautiful, Iris. In a dress, in tactical gear, or naked, I would guess, too. Don't dismiss your charms."

For a few beats, she searched his gaze. The uncertainty made him want to find the bastard who'd dented her confidence.

Oh, Iris could charge into any mission or assignment without hesitation. However, there was more to a person than just their job, and Antony silently vowed to tell her how gorgeous she was until she truly believed it.

Reluctantly, he released her hand. As much as he wanted to devote the night to that goal, he couldn't miss this meeting. He said, "I will come back to this, I promise. For now, let's go. We have to get to the pub and make sure everything is ready for the meeting."

And as she walked ahead of him out the door, he

swore she swished her skirt and exaggerated the sway of her hips on purpose. Thankfully, once he waited for her to go onto the street, she resumed her normal walk. *Good.* He didn't want any competition later.

Once enough time had passed, Antony headed out and toward the old pub, doing his best to clear his head along the way. The informant was risking everything to meet him, and he couldn't fuck it up.

Iris fucking hated dresses. She usually only wore them for special occasions, when traditional dragon-shifter clothes were required.

However, when Antony had come out of the bedroom and looked at her as if he wanted to eat up every inch, she'd started to wonder if she'd underestimated the power of dresses. Because if it could make Antony Holbrook, who she thought might be one of the most powerful men in the country—albeit behind closed doors—speechless and his jaw drop, she imagined it could work well in enemy situations, too.

Although she doubted she'd shiver at a stranger's gaze. No, she'd probably want to knee them in the bollocks.

And yet, when Antony had given her a slow once-over, her skin had heated, and she'd barely restrained herself from teasing him by lifting her skirt a few inches.

Would his incredible control have snapped? Would he have calmly wooed her into more?

Not for the first time, she admitted she wanted to know Antony better. Much better.

However, as she stood behind Antony's nameless technician in a little flat across the street from an old pub, she willed herself to focus. Antony was counting on her to be ready, if he needed her knowledge or help.

Her dragon snorted. *If you had jumped him yesterday, then you wouldn't be so randy now.*

With everything going on, you're still focused on sex?

Aye. It's been a while.

Iris ignored her beast to focus on the screen. Antony wore a hidden camera in the button of his shirt, and he'd entered the pub. He moved through a crowd of people toward the bar. After ordering a pint, he sat in a corner booth and chatted with some passing people.

Well, two females, to be exact.

A shot of jealousy roared through her, and her dragon spoke up. *Yes, he's ours. Just admit it.*

Not now, dragon. I need to help him.

Her beast harrumphed. *Fine. But later, don't run away from him if he flirts. Embrace it.*

She ignored her beast since the latest female had left and a male wearing builder's clothes—the sweatshirt had the company name, and his trousers and boots were well worn—motioned toward the empty space across from Antony. "Any fan of the Spurs here is a friend of mine. We should stick together."

Ah, so that's why Antony had worn a Tottenham Spurs scarf in Inverness, whose team was the Caledonian Thistle F.C.

They chatted about football for a bit before the match started and the attention in the pub shifted to the TVs. It was then that Antony and the other male started talking in quiet tones.

But his microphone was excellent, so Iris heard everything.

Antony asked, "Any luck landing that job you wanted?"

During the drive to Inverness, Antony had explained some of their code. He was asking if the male had discovered any of the dragon hunter prisons or research facilities. While Clan Stonefire's head Protector, Kai, had found a few, they'd been smaller. Antony suspected there were larger ones, maybe inside abandoned properties or mines.

The male replied, "I think so. But Birkwood Castle is a bit far from Inverness, so I'll have to check with my girlfriend to see if I can take it or not."

Iris racked her brain for the place. She'd heard the name somewhere...then remembered about the abandoned manor house that had been bought to turn into a hotel, given up, bought again, and currently sat empty. And was supposedly haunted.

But maybe it was a ruse—being supposedly haunted could be a brilliant tactic to keep others away.

Iris wanted to race out of the room to head south—

Birkwood Castle was in Scotland, but south of Glasgow —and check it out. But Antony's next words kept her in place. "What renovations do they want to do? If it pays well, it might be worth it."

"Aye, well, they want to turn it into a fancy retreat facility, last I heard. Quite the change going from a mental hospital for decades to a fancy retreat."

"Retreat for what?"

"Pregnant mothers."

The human sipped his pint, and Iris wondered if it was really that simple. Maybe the female dragons were there, already being used for breeding, and anger rushed through her. While she couldn't understand anyone hating humans enough to abandon their clans, she'd seen reports about what Stonefire and even Snowridge had discovered in some of the previous research facilities. About how the Dragon Knights had forced pregnancies on the female dragon-shifters.

No one deserved that, but especially not Zoe. Not her clan member.

Antony and the human male cheered at something in the game and then went on to talk about players and World Cups and other things two blokes in a pub would discuss.

Even though she kept an ear out in case Antony might need her help, they never talked about anything but sports after that.

She shouldn't feel useless, and yet she did. Not wanting to waste time, she asked the tech to bring up everything he could about Birkwood Castle. Because as soon as Antony left the pub, they were going to return to the house to discuss strategy and leave as soon as possible to investigate their new lead.

By the time Antony could leave the pub without attracting notice—the end of the bloody match—he was itching to dash back to his secure flat. The informant hadn't said much after mentioning Birkwood Castle, but there had been little drips here and there, if one knew the code.

He suspected some of the missing female dragons might be at the old manor house. However, they wouldn't be in the building itself, which was derelict, but rather underneath it.

And since the dragon hunters had once inhabited an extensive network of tunnels, back before the Dragon Knights had started taking the spotlight off the hunters, it was entirely plausible they were using them again. Or maybe had never fully abandoned them.

So many flies to swat down, and Antony never seemed to have enough resources.

By the time he reached the safe house, he noticed the lights were on. But as agreed, one side of the curtains was open on the first floor and the curtains in the window below were open on the other side. The signal that Iris was there.

Regardless, Antony was still careful about approaching the back door and entering. Once he'd locked the door, he silently crept up the stairs and into the flat until he could see Iris staring down at a map. He knocked against the door trim, and she glanced over. Her hair was still up, but she'd changed to jeans and a T-shirt. Ones that hugged her arse and hips in a lovely way.

But even though he wanted to smile, charm, and kiss her, he forced himself to stride over and ask, "What more did you find out?"

For a second, relief flashed in her eyes. As if she'd been unsure of how he'd act now.

Resisting the urge to curse anyone who'd made her feel lesser, he focused on her reply as she tapped the map. "The small town of Lesmahagow is near Birkwood Castle, but not too close. The town to the northeast and the golf course to the south of the castle are our two biggest obstacles. I would've researched more about security and any videos online about the place, but there's no internet in here."

"No, it's a security precaution. Whilst my team relies a lot on technology, there are a lot of pitfalls. Regardless, my tech guy has already contacted a trusted few under me, and we should know more by tomorrow morning."

Iris stood. "We should leave now and find somewhere to stay closer to Birkwood. That way, we can act quicker once we have enough information."

"Ah, I think not, my dear. It's better to remain here,

investigating what else we can find out about Jude and even Zoe's disappearance, before rushing into things. Kai and Trina have already been reassigned to scout the area, and since Kai has some experience with finding dragon hunter tunnels, I thought it best to send him out ahead."

"And us? Why do we need to stay here? Surely you have some staff who could investigate Jude."

He risked tracing her cheek, oh-so-slowly. Her breath hitched as her pupils flashed to slits and back, and he smiled. "We both need some rest. Besides, staying in one place for a day or two has its benefits."

Antony continued caressing her cheek, wanting more, much more, but not wanting to push Iris too far.

Eventually she replied, "Just rest, aye?"

"If that's all you want."

She bit her bottom lip, and his gaze shot to her mouth. Damn, he wanted to take that bottom lip between his teeth and tug.

Iris stepped back, turned around, and braced her hands on the table. For a beat, then another, she said nothing. But Antony was patient, so he stayed in place.

Her voice was lower when she said, "I can't risk it."

"Risk what?"

"Losing focus. Or my spot for this assignment."

"Your spot is ensured, even if you need to work with one of my colleagues instead of me. I can even call my brother to work with you instead, since investigating old ruins is sort of his specialty anyway."

She shook her head, but didn't turn around. "No, it's not that. As you mentioned, I'm good at my job and you wouldn't want to kick me off of this." She glanced at him. "And that is why I can't risk anything with you. I can't have any distractions."

He dared a step and sighed inwardly with relief when Iris didn't bolt. "I think it's more than that."

Her eyebrows drew together. "What are you blathering about now?"

"It's not blather, my dear. And I understand—you're afraid. But so am I. The last time I let anyone close, it ended in disaster. And yet, you're brilliant and beautiful and you understand what I've done the past twenty years, of what I've had to sacrifice, more than most." He took another step closer. "It's because of how wonderful you are that I'm willing to take a chance, Iris." He leaned his face a few inches closer, inhaling her sweet scent of jasmine and pure woman. "Are you willing to do the same?"

And so he waited to see how Iris responded. Even if she ran, he wasn't going to give up that easily. For the first time in a long time, there was a future he wanted. And as long as he thought Iris wanted it too, he would go after it.

Chapter Fifteen

I ris stared into Antony's brown eyes, wanting to believe the truth and desire and longing she saw there.

And yet, he'd spent the last two decades living in the shadows, pretending to be other people on demand. It could be an act. Plus, he was handsome enough to snag just about any female he wanted.

So why did he want her so badly?

Her dragon growled. *Don't do that. Don't make excuses. You want him, too, but are scared.*

Aye, I'm scared. Of being pushed off this assignment. Or, if not, then I'll be sidelined to a safe job, far away from the danger.

Just because he's stubborn and strong and commanding sometimes doesn't mean he's going to become an overprotective dragon-shifter, aye? Let alone feel hurt if you do better than him at something.

I believed that once before with a human. Why would it be any different this time?

He isn't our ex. Antony is ten times that male.

"Iris."

She jolted from her thoughts and focused back on Antony. He tilted his head, studying her, and part of her wanted to say fuck it, and run into his arms. To take a chance, and for once feel desired and treasured and yet still respected as an equal.

He said, "Since you aren't wearing Dr. Turner's dragon-thought voice contraption, you're going to have to talk to me. What's racing through your head? Or maybe I should guess?"

Wanting a wee bit of a distraction, she replied, "What's your guess?"

He tapped his finger against his chin a second before saying, "Well, there's what I hope you're thinking about and what you're probably actually thinking about. I want you and your dragon to come up with some more of those fantasies, featuring me and you naked. However, you're probably thinking of reasons to run away and stay safe."

Her dragon snorted. *I like what he wants us to be thinking about better.*

Of course you would.

Iris hesitated, which was out of character for her. And yet, she'd been hurt badly. Aye, it'd been over a decade ago, but some wounds still smarted.

Paul's angry words at her last promotion still

haunted her: *People like you are the reason the British Army is going to shite. Publicity is better than promoting true merit. So fuck your breakup, Iris. I only ever went after you because my mates bet me to shag a dragon-shifter. The sex was good enough to pretend to date you. But now, I'm going to do everything I can to ruin your career.*

Even though Paul had eventually been kicked out of the army for drunkenness and lewd behavior, Iris had spent so many years trying to prove that she deserved everything she got. She worked twice as hard as any of the males, just in case. Sacrificing friends and even time with her family in the process.

But maybe, just maybe, after a while, it'd become a shield. A comfortable, familiar one that now hindered her rather than helped her.

Her dragon's voice was softer as she said, *Antony isn't a young male, trying to prove himself. He realizes that a strong female isn't a threat, but an asset. Don't shut him out completely.*

Before she could think better of it, Iris blurted, "I can't promise that I won't back off, or get scared, or keep trying to push you away when things get intense. However..."

Antony took a step toward her, but Iris didn't back away. "However what?"

"I-I like you, Antony. More than I should."

He took another step. "Like as in fancy? Or like as in friend?"

"A bit of both?"

He smiled. "I like that answer. But what happens next, if anything, is up to you. We can retire to separate rooms to study maps and what we have on Jude so far, to prep for tomorrow. We'll focus solely on the job for as long as you need to." He took another step. "I can be patient, but if you want anything more, even just a little, then tell me, Iris."

Her heart thumped harder inside her chest as she scanned his gaze. He wanted her—he wasn't trying to hide it.

Her dragon spoke up. *Just lay the ground rules. No kissing on the mouth until you're possibly ready for it.*

But can he manage that? In my limited experience, males lose their minds as soon as they're naked.

This is Antony. Stop making excuses and just talk to him.

Iris swallowed, clenched and unclenched her fingers, and whispered, "I need you to promise something before I say anything else."

He tilted his head. "What?"

"You know dragon-shifters, which means you know how fated mates work. I can't risk kissing you and starting a mate-claim frenzy. So that means no kissing on the mouth, aye? Can you handle it?"

He smiled. "There's a lot I can kiss without touching your mouth, my dear. It's a challenge, one that I look forward to."

Even though his words sent a rush of heat through

her body, she still rolled her eyes. "Your cheesy charm never goes away?"

He chuckled. "I'm afraid not. Besides, it makes your heart race and pupils flash, so I think you like it."

She frowned. "Your hearing can't be good enough to know when my heart rate kicks up."

He closed the distance between them and lightly caressed her neck, right where her blood pumped under the skin. "No, but this tells me all I need to know."

Each pass of his warm, rough finger against her skin made her heart race faster. Staring into his eyes, she sucked in a breath at the desire blazing there.

He murmured, "Yes, I want you, Iris. I have for a while, to the point I was jealous of my brother, even after he found his mate." Leaning down, he nuzzled her neck. "I don't know how other men have been fools for so long and haven't tried to win you, but it's to my advantage." He nipped where her neck and shoulder met, and Iris quickly gripped his upper arms to stay standing. He whispered, "Tell me what you want, Iris. And do say it's me."

She chuckled at his teasing, arrogant words. "You never stop, aye?"

"No." He nipped her earlobe. "But just know that with you, it's different." He leaned back until he met her eyes again. "With you, I'm doing my best not to pretend. Sometimes it'll be difficult, given how I've worn a mask for so long. But I'm trying, and maybe with you I can finally figure out the real me."

Iris burned to kiss him, but instead lifted a hand and traced his jaw. When Antony closed his eyes and leaned into her touch, she smiled. For all his gadgets and power and secrets, he was still just a male.

Her dragon spoke up. *Then what are you waiting for? Strip him and ride him. Hard.*

Ignoring her beast, she ran her other hand up Antony's chest until she could trace the pulsing artery in his neck. "Aye, I see what you mean about not needing supersensitive hearing to notice a racing heart. Something I've never really had to pay attention to before."

His eyes opened, and he said, "Well, those of us at a disadvantage must learn other ways of matching your skills."

"Disadvantage, says the male with all the techno gadgets."

"I knew showing them would impress you and help my case."

She rolled her eyes. "They're nice, aye? But since most of them are useless to me in my dragon form, they're not really *that* impressive."

His fingers traced her cheek. "Then I must find other ways to awe you, my dear. Ways that involve your legs spread and my mouth too busy to charm with words."

A rush of heat shot through her body, and yet Iris wasn't quite ready to end the playfulness. Something she hadn't experienced with anyone in a long, long time.

So she snorted. "I somehow think you'll still find a way to talk. You're not the silent type, aye?"

He quirked an eyebrow. "I can be. But I don't want to be with you, Iris. I don't want to hide."

As she searched his gaze, she saw nothing but truth. Aye, he could be lying—he was a professional. And yet, her gut said he wasn't.

Iris also realized how tired she was of hiding herself, of always having to try harder just to avoid being criticized.

Her dragon spoke up. *Stop thinking and just tell him aye, we want him. We want to give him a chance.*

She stepped closer, wrapped her arms around Antony's neck and opened her mouth to do exactly that when someone knocked on the front door.

Antony cursed, and she tamped down her irritation as she asked, "Were you expecting someone?"

"No. And whoever the bloody hell it is better have a good reason for coming." He quickly kissed her cheek, the touch fleeting, before charging toward the door. After checking through the peephole, he opened it to reveal a human male Iris didn't recognize.

Antony did, though, and ushered him inside. Only once he'd shut the door did he ask, "What's going on?"

He glanced at Iris, and Antony waved a hand toward her. "She can hear anything you have to say."

The unknown male stated, "We found Jude."

Iris reached the males just as Antony said, "Don't make me ask for more."

The human male nodded. "Right, well, he's dead. He was found in one of the canals in Manchester. I managed to get the case turned over to us and confiscated all the evidence. However, there wasn't much. The water destroyed most of it."

Maybe Iris should let Antony handle this, but her instincts kicked in and she blurted, "What did you find?"

Antony discreetly brushed his pinky against hers and gave a nearly imperceptible nod. He approved.

It shouldn't mean so much, and yet it did.

Her dragon sighed. *I told you he's different.*

Iris focused on the other human's reply as he said, "His neck was sliced. Not with a knife, but rather a dragon's talon."

Iris cursed as Antony said, "But I'd lay everything that it wasn't done by an actual dragon-shifter. Regardless of Jude's betrayal, he was technically the DDA liaison and one of the last people a dragon would attack. The talon could be from a dead dragon, though."

The male nodded. "I think so, too. The incision is large, meaning someone was in their full dragon form and not partially shifted. And there weren't any reported dragon sightings in Manchester recently, either."

Iris spoke up. "There's a wee chance a dragon killed him and then moved him to the city via a car, but it would be a hell of a lot of work to do so."

Antony nodded. "I agree. Stephen, did you bring the initial reports with you?"

The male took out a flash drive and handed it over. "It's all on here, with the usual protections."

Even though she wanted to ask what they were, she focused on the bigger picture. "Did a human find him?"

"Unfortunately, yes. But as far as I can tell, there aren't any photos or video on the internet."

"At least not yet," Iris muttered.

Stephen shrugged. "It's the world we live in now. People love true crime and gory photos."

Antony waved a hand in dismissal. "I have a team who will scour and delete, as necessary. As for the body, I want Dr. Turner to work on the autopsy and see if she can find anything to help us. If even a tiny sliver of the talon is still in the skin, she should be able to extract DNA and go from there. I want you to work with her and do whatever she asks."

The male sighed. "And I thought you liked me, Holbrook."

Antony snorted. "Just try not to upset her again. I don't need more messes to clean up."

"I'll do my best."

After a few last comments, the male left. Antony leaned against the door and crossed his arms over his chest. "Well, it seems as if we'll be going to Birkwood Castle after all. Four hours of sleep and then we'll pack up and leave."

Iris studied him, wondering if "business as usual" was his way of brushing off earlier.

But then he walked over, kissed her cheek, and whispered, "We, sadly, don't have enough time for that. But think of it this way—I now have time to think about how to drive you wild and make you scream even louder."

"Antony."

He nuzzled her neck, and Iris gripped his arms. Somehow, this male always made her knees weak.

Which was both irritating and exciting.

Her dragon spoke up. *Who needs sleep?*

Antony does. We napped. He didn't.

Her beast sighed but then kept silent.

He leaned back, traced her lips with a finger, and she resisted a shiver as he said, "Sweet dreams, Iris. Selfish as I am, I hope they're of me."

As he waggled his eyebrows, she burst out laughing.

He whispered, "I love your laugh. You definitely need to do it more often."

Before she could think of how to respond, he walked away and entered his bedroom.

Iris moved to the sofa and plopped down, placing a hand over her racing heart.

Her dragon finally spoke again. *Maybe if we give him a shot of dragon's blood, he won't need much sleep?*

Dragon, no.

No for now? Or no until later?

Maybe I'll ask Dr. Turner about it. But for now, he needs to sleep, and so do we. I have a feeling the next few days or weeks are going to be intense and exhausting.

Try not to wear him out too much. We have to share him, aye?

She bit back a laugh. *Naughty dragon. Stop it. I mean with the case, not sex.*

Her beast sniffed. *If you say so.*

Iris's brain raced with everything that had happened over the last few days, still unsure of *how* Antony Holbrook had chipped away at her walls so quickly.

However, she used her training as best as she could to pack away anything unrelated to finding who was behind the dead dragon-shifters, the dead human, and the kidnapped females. She needed to find Zoe, sooner rather than later.

And it worked. At least until she fell asleep, when she dreamed of what might've happened if that male hadn't knocked on the door and interrupted her moment with Antony.

Chapter Sixteen

After two days of watching the other female dragon-shifters, Zoe was starting to notice alliances. Namely, the ones who wanted to trust that she would help them and those who viewed her as a traitor for not hating humans. Most of the latter group were also open to Chelsea's plan of dragon world domination. A few trusted no one but themselves.

Her cousin, Rebecca, was on the fence about whom to believe. She rarely talked with Zoe, yet she kept stealing glances, as if wanting to learn more, but was afraid to.

Zoe nearly reached out to her dragon but stopped since she was still silent. She missed her inner beast more than anything else.

However, the lack of their second half was hard for any dragon-shifter, and it was an angle she'd been testing out with the others. Because Zoe doubted their captors would ever let them have their beasts back, and even though everyone probably knew that on some level, voicing it had made a few females less hostile toward her.

Some, though, said Chelsea would find a way to bring back their inner beasts once they escaped.

Rubbing her forehead, Zoe resisted sighing. Bloody hell, she'd never envisioned having to play politics like this. And yet, if she ever wanted to get free, she would have to.

As she mentally went through the list of females she wanted to talk with today, Bethan, the Welsh dragon in her cell, said, "You still haven't said why they put you in here with us."

"That's because I don't know."

"Right, I'm sure you don't."

Zoe rolled her eyes. "Believe me or not, I don't care. As I said, I was meeting a DDA liaison and the next thing I knew, I ended up here." Thankfully, she'd regained her strength, so she stood and studied Bethan. "How did *you* end up in here?"

Silence.

That was something no one had wanted to discuss, along with Zoe's news about the mass grave. Some still refused to believe her, although she thought it might be because of denial rather than true disbelief.

Zoe shrugged. "Aye, well, then there's not much else to discuss."

The female fell silent, and Zoe pretended to study

her nails as she checked out the cell across from hers. Her biggest conquest so far was the female formerly from Skyhunter named Gemma. Even so, the female hadn't revealed much beyond how someone had shot canisters of something into their settlement back in the Cairngorms. And then she'd woken up here.

Zoe was starting to think there had been two types of gas—one to knock out everyone and allow someone to take the females of childbearing age, and another to kill the rest.

And to think, she'd been on a treasure hunt with Logan Lamont and Emma MacAllister not too long ago, and now she was trying to convince traitors to trust her.

Bethan went to her bunk and turned her back, feigning sleep. Zoe was about to talk with Gemma again, to see if she could learn even more, when her cousin walked over to her and said, "I believe you were meeting with that DDA person."

Hiding her surprise, she replied, "Why?"

Rebecca frowned. "What do you mean, why?"

"Why now and not before?"

Her cousin lowered her voice. "It's the most likely scenario. Even if I didn't agree with Finn about the humans, I can't imagine him imprisoning all of us and putting you in here, too, to find out information."

"It would be rather elaborate, aye? And expensive." She studied Rebecca a beat and decided to push a wee bit. After walking to the corner, she waited for Rebecca to follow before lowering her voice so no one else should be able to hear. "Who would want to put us all together, then?"

Emotions flitted across her cousin's face—uncertainty, worry, fear, and finally resignation. As if she'd made a decision.

Zoe might be one of the younger Protectors, but she had learned a while ago when to keep silent and when to talk. And so she waited.

Eventually, Rebecca leaned over to her ear and whispered so softly Zoe almost missed it. "When they moved us in here, I had started to wake up." She paused, and Zoe didn't even dare to breathe until her cousin spoke again. "They mentioned a 'she' was in charge. Someone named Green. Do you know who that is?"

A female named Green? Then it hit her—Margot Green was Simon Bourne's half-sister. Bourne was in charge of the dragon hunters, and recently, Margot had caused some trouble for Stonefire. Zoe's gut said that was the "she" they'd referred to, which meant Bourne's sister was a bigger threat than they'd first surmised.

Zoe's triumph at learning the information was quickly replaced with anger. Had the rogue dragon-shifters kept their people in the dark about possible enemies? Even if they believed humans were beneath them, the dragon hunters had dangerous weapons that could hurt or fatally wound dragon-shifters. And they should've been warned.

But before she could prod for more information, the daily lunch arrived. The human males who delivered it wore masks, like always, and didn't say a word as they pushed small troughs into each cell. Her cousin went to grab a sandwich—no one had been poisoned...yet—and Zoe lost her chance to ask more questions.

However, she'd learned something extremely important. So as she watched everyone eat, she went through what she knew about Simon Bourne, his sister, the dragon hunters, and anything else she could use to better understand their captors. Because understanding them would be the key to escaping, or at least give her a way to signal to her clan members where she was.

Over the next day, as Iris spent more time with Antony, she became more and more impressed. He had a knack for talking with informants and allies, smoothly transitioning from small talk to vital information, all while charming people along the way. He might be cocky, but he should be. Iris would never have the skill of coaxing someone to share more information like he could. Or suffer through small talk long enough to look natural before learning what she really wanted to know.

Since she wore the special contacts that hid her flashing dragon eyes—she was in a town near Birkwood Castle, discreetly watching Antony's back—her dragon spoke up. *We have better observation and tracking skills. Don't compare. That way lies madness.*

Aye, I know. Now, hush. I've seen that male walk by twice before.

She sipped her coffee, watching as the human male slowed down his pace as he passed Antony talking to a female informant. The female ran the local florist shop, was in her sixties, and kept touching Antony's arm. But whenever she did, Antony made a quip, and she laughed.

As the female did it again, Iris ignored her to watch the male. He dropped something a few feet from where Antony was standing and quickly strode away. Antony had seen it, though, and discreetly kicked it into the street. Once it rolled to a stop, a few seconds passed before it released a tiny amount of gas, one she could see because of her keen eyesight.

Damn, someone was on to them.

Antony ushered the female inside her shop. Iris itched to investigate the small object in the street, but knew someone—or many someones—were waiting and watching for exactly that.

So she stayed put, leisurely finishing her drink and muffin before finally leaving the small cafe. She deliberately walked away from the small object and down the route she and Antony had agreed upon earlier. Except at the hidden meeting spot in a nearby forest, she didn't find Antony but his younger brother, Max.

The blond-haired human lacked his battered fedora today, though, and wore almost normal looking clothes in jeans and a button-down shirt. He tugged at his sleeves—

an action that reminded her of Antony—before he spotted her. He winked and waited for her to get close enough before he murmured, "My brother called in the cavalry, and so here I am."

She blinked. "For what?"

"The local council is thinking of tearing down Birkwood Castle, but first needs an archaeologist to take a look. Since some records say a dragon-shifter village existed there over a thousand years ago, there might be something of historical significance, near or under it. And as you know, I'm quite famous for dragon-shifter archaeology these days."

Max had recently discovered Dragon's Court, an extensive dragon-shifter piece of history, with his dragon mate, Lavinia. The pair and their discovery had been everywhere in the news and online. "Aye, well, that still doesn't explain why you're here in this forest and not your brother."

"You used to love me, Iris. What happened?"

She muttered, "I miss the clown you used to be."

Max grinned. "In public, I still am, sometimes. But things will move faster if I get to the point and not ramble about the finer points of Roman mosaics for an hour."

"Aye, good point. So get to it."

Max shrugged. "You're to be my security guard. That's all I know."

Iris checked the secure phone Antony had given her. There was a brief message: *Be patient. Go with him.*

After trying to read between the lines for so many years, cynical Iris thought it was a ploy to get her away from danger. And yet, Antony loved his brother, and she wanted to believe he'd picked her because of how much Max meant to him.

Pushing her cynicism away, she gestured down a path, one that led to the car Antony had given her to use. "How did you get roped in so quickly?"

"My brother has helped me a lot over the years, but he rarely calls in a favor. So when he asked, I couldn't say no." He studied Iris a beat before adding, "My brother sings your praises now. Said if he couldn't watch over me, then you're the next best thing."

Ignoring the thrill at Antony's compliment, she drawled, "Probably because I know how you can wander off and get into trouble."

"Well, I had to be a convincing fool. I'll probably wander a bit this time, too, just to make it authentic."

Even though she shouldn't venture into anything personal—because Max might then ask her something too—she couldn't help but ask, "Your mate must be exhausted by the double life, aye?"

A soft look came over Max's face. "Lavinia gets to play up scolding me in public and has a lot of fun with it. Maybe one day I can drop the act entirely. However, when we're alone, we get to be ourselves." He raised an eyebrow. "Given how much my brother talks about you now, my guess is that he gets to be himself with you."

Damn Max and his perceptiveness. "I don't know what you mean."

"Suit yourself. But just don't hurt my brother, Iris. He's been through a lot, as I'm sure you know by now, and he deserves a little happiness. More than painting cats and dogs and watching other people experience joy at his efforts, but never sharing it with him."

Iris could lie and say she couldn't hurt Antony because there was nothing there.

And yet, Max was showing his true colors with her, no longer hiding like he did with most of the world.

Her dragon spoke up. *I've always rather liked him. Even if I miss his other persona, his true colors show more of how he and Antony are a lot alike in some ways.*

Except that Antony is a lot more attractive. And charismatic. And clever.

Good to see the last two days haven't changed your mind about giving him a chance.

After the car ride down to southern Scotland, they'd spent all of their time meeting with Kai and Trina, as well as figuring out plans.

The car ride had been full of sexual tension. Every time Antony had accidentally touched her, her heart rate had kicked up. And when she'd done the same, he'd also reacted.

And yet, there had never been a moment to explore more.

She replied to her dragon. *No, I haven't changed my mind. And I never would've guessed that wanting to bed a male would be such a strong motivation for finishing a job.*

Her beast sniffed. *Well, we never met a male like Antony before.*

Max's voice prevented her from replying to her beast. "You must be wearing those contacts my brother talked about. I don't like them. Flashing dragon eyes help me better understand when to talk or not."

Her dragon remained silent as Iris unlocked the car doors and gestured them inside. Once they were seated, she replied, "Well, I'll have to pretend to be a human security guard, so I have no choice, aye?"

Once she was on the road, heading back toward Lesmahagow near Birkwood Castle, Max spoke again. "So, does my brother drop his mask around you?"

She raised an eyebrow but kept her eyes on the road. "I could refuse to answer."

Max grinned. "You could, but I don't think you will. Because I can go on about the mural found near Dragon's Court, the hidden secrets, and how we found it. I mean, some of the mosaic-like art was bloody amazing. It must've taken forever to—"

Iris sighed. "You're playing that part again, are you?"

"Hey, you said you missed it."

Iris gripped the steering wheel tighter, released her fingers a little, and gripped it again. Her dragon spoke up. *Think of it this way—you can also learn more about Antony by telling Max a wee bit.*

Aye, I know, dragon. But that means talking about myself.

He won't use things against you, like our ex-arsehole. Max has always gone on about how brilliant a flyer we are.

Of course you remember that.

Just talk with him.

Iris glanced over at Max, who was studying her. He said, "You were talking with your dragon. You have a tell."

She frowned. "What the bloody hell are you talking about?"

"Your mouth twitches up and down, depending on whether you agree or disagree. Or, at least, that's my theory."

For all that she'd been told about how Max had once worked for his brother, she'd never really believed it. Until now. "I'm not sure about that, but I'll have to be more careful in the future."

He waved a hand in dismissal. "We're nearly family, and I would never betray you like that."

Panic surged in her chest. "Listen, I don't know what Antony told you—"

"No, no, nothing like that. You and I have spent a lot of time together over the years, is all. And now we're working together again. If not family, then I'd like to think we're friends."

A year ago, Iris would've snorted at the concept.

And yet, she'd let down her guard bit by bit with the formerly clueless human. And now that she knew him a wee bit better, and sort of fancied his brother, she didn't want to push Max away.

"Friends. Sort of. But don't expect me to bail your arse out in the middle of the night."

"Oh, I have a mate and we're rather busy at night. Well, until the baby arrives, at any rate."

"That's right, I forgot about that. I'm surprised you would leave Lavinia alone."

He snorted. "Lavinia doesn't want to stay in bed and be pampered. It drives her mad. But Antony has people watching over her on Skyhunter and at the dig site, so I know she'll be okay for a few days. She's the one who convinced me to come to Scotland."

That's right—Max and his mate had moved to Clan Skyhunter, in the south of England. "Seeing as we're friends now, tell me about Dr. Turner and your brother, aye?"

"Not the most deft change of topic. However, I truly don't know Antony's secret plans, or team members, or projects. So, sorry, I can't help you. Dr. Turner is nice enough. She even told us we're having a daughter, despite the silly dragon-shifter tradition of waiting."

She could push, but decided not to. Max was trying to be her friend, and she needed to stay on topic and not constantly change it. However, she wasn't good at chatting about bairns, and she blurted the first thing she could think of. "A female bairn? Well, the theory of a human male father and a female dragon-shifter mother having a greater chance of producing females seems to be true."

"Seems so. So if Antony ends up your true mate, you'll probably have a daughter as well. If you hurry, they'll be close in age!"

She gripped the steering wheel tighter. "I can't determine who's my true mate, as you well know. And I'm certainly not planning out bairns."

"Either way, you'll need to help train my daughter. Given me and Lavinia are her parents, she'll probably have an adventurous spirit, and I'd rather she be able to defend herself."

Iris smiled. "Aye, maybe I can do that. If you convince other dragon parents to let me do the same."

"Out to change the world, I see. I'll work on it. Now, ask me."

"Ask you what?"

"Oh, come on, Iris. You're burning to ask me about Antony. He's nowhere near as brilliant as me, of course, but he's still a great catch."

"I see that cockiness runs in the family."

"It's not cocky if it's true."

She snorted. "You two *are* more alike than I'd realized."

"Your window to ask questions is going away in three, two—"

"And you're back to being annoying." Max shrugged, held up three fingers, and started counting down again. So she blurted, "How are you so close, given the age difference?"

He frowned. "Antony didn't tell you? Well, that is rather personal and you can ask him about the details. All I'll say is that he raised me once our parents died."

"So you're giving me just enough to be interested, so I'll ask your brother?"

"That's the plan. Is it working?"

She shook her head. "How about we discuss your survey plans instead?"

Max sighed. "You're no fun, but fine. What do you want to know?"

And as Max went over his plans for Birkwood Castle, Iris kept wanting to ask more about Antony raising Max. Especially since Antony had gone through a lot of tragedy with his ex-fiancée, and now she'd learned of this. Had he suffered even more when his parents died? Most likely after losing his female, given the ten or so years between Antony and Max.

Her dragon spoke up. *At least we had our parents.*

Iris had often been irritated by her mum and dad. Her mother had wanted her to attend university, maybe even become a doctor, but Iris had never wanted that future. Her father had been slightly more understanding, but still had wanted her to do something less dangerous than clan security.

190

However, just thinking of them dying in her early twenties made her heart squeeze.

More than ever, she wanted to finish this bloody investigation, rescue Zoe, and have the time to learn more about Antony Holbrook and see if he could be a male she trusted not to hurt her.

Chapter Seventeen

Antony had just finished talking with Dr. Turner about the gas released in the street when a key turned in the lock of the flat's door. This place had an outer door and a series of inner door "flats" that were dummies. And since only a handful of people had access via the palm print scanner outside his location, he didn't reach for the weapon in his lap.

Max walked through, with Iris right behind him, and Antony relaxed. "I hope you're not expecting me to cook, Max."

His brother grinned and came to meet him. "You're a shite cook, anyway." He raised some bags. "I nabbed us some food, so we don't starve. Because Iris said whilst she can cook, she's not going to."

Antony finally met Iris's gaze, and a mixture of relief and desire rushed through him. He'd hated not being able to meet her in the forest. He was aware that she could take care of herself, and yet, after talking with Dr. Turner, Antony was a teensy bit more worried about their enemies.

Iris cleared her throat and moved to stand next to Max. "Aye, well, I'd rather work on finding Zoe and the others. Please tell me you have some news. Max didn't find much today during his initial walk around Birkwood Castle, and I need to think about something other than dirt layers and what they mean."

Antony quirked an eyebrow at his brother. "The obsessed archaeologist came out again, then?"

His brother shrugged and headed toward the small kitchen. "It's what they expect of me. Besides, like Iris said, I didn't find much." He put one of the bags on the counter and then went to stand by the door. "However, I don't need to hear all the details. To be honest, it's probably safer for me if I don't. Have a nice dinner, you two. Maybe light a candle or two to set the mood."

Max winked and exited the room before Antony could scold him.

He'd told his blasted brother not to interfere. But then again, Max didn't always listen if he thought he knew better.

Something else they had in common.

Iris unpacked the food, and he went to help. For about a minute, they worked in silence. But it wasn't strained. No, it was more...domestic and comfortable and something he'd once dreamed of having, but thought that had died with Lisa.

He envisioned him and Iris living together, doing this every night, and he smiled. Iris's voice broke through his dreams. "Why are you smiling at me like that?"

"I was just daydreaming."

She arched an eyebrow. "Daydreaming? The great Antony Holbrook?"

Even though he should focus on what he'd learned and their shared enemies and the mission, he couldn't help but reach out and tickle her side. Iris yelped, moved away, and glared. "That wasn't fair."

"Why not, my dear?"

"Don't 'my dear' me right now. You still haven't told me what happened after I left the town."

"And I will, as soon as we sit down to eat. You can take a few minutes to unwind."

"Being tickled is unwinding?"

He raised his arms and gestured toward his sides. "Come try and find out."

"Some of us are adults."

"Oh, come on, Iris. You know you want to. Besides, then we'll be even. Think of it that way."

She glanced down at his chest and Antony resisted undoing his buttons to tease her some more. He wanted to bring out the slightly playful version of Iris, the one he rarely saw but knew existed.

He twirled once and said, "Your chance is going away in ten, nine, eight..."

As he counted down, he wondered if he'd misjudged the situation. But in the blink of an eye, Iris rushed over and danced her fingers along his ribs. Antony barked out a laugh and tried to move away. When she followed, he gently took hold of her wrists and stared into her dark brown eyes.

Her hot breath danced across his face, making desire rush through him, straight to his cock. What he wouldn't give to be able to lift her to the counter, spread her thighs, and make her relax even further. Well, mostly, until she started digging her nails into his scalp and begging for release.

"Antony."

"Yes, Iris?"

Her gaze searched his, and he almost missed the dance of emotions there—uncertainty, worry, desire, and yearning.

So she wanted him just as much as he wanted her.

Leaning in, he nuzzled her cheek. "Tell me what you want, Iris." He kissed her neck. "Ask me for anything."

He released her wrists, and her hands gripped his shoulders. After a beat, he ran his fingers down her sides. Slowly, inch by inch, and this time, she sucked in a breath instead of laughing.

"I want..."

Her voice died down as he moved to nuzzle her other cheek. "Yes?" Antony moved back until he could see her eyes again. For once, her guard was down. The soft, heated look made him want to growl.

And yet, Iris had been hurt. Badly. There would come a time when he didn't need to be so patient. However, she wasn't quite there yet.

Since her pupils didn't flash, it meant she still had the blasted contacts in. And yet, he swore she was talking with her dragon.

As he lightly caressed her hip, he waited to see if his dragonwoman was ready for more. He could wait if he had to. But Antony hoped he could finally see her gorgeous naked body, drink in every inch, and start winning her with more than words.

Iris had fully planned on avoiding Antony's childish games to focus on the mission.

However, at his twirling and showing the playful side he usually hid from the world, she hadn't wanted him to bottle things up and go back to being secret agent Antony.

So she'd tickled him. And when he'd taken her wrists, a thrill shot through her. Not fear. Oh, no, far from it. Desire and need and wanting.

And now he waited for her to say what she wanted.

Her dragon spoke up. *Tell him to strip. I want to see him. Then he can undress us and help us relax.*

I can't risk him kissing us on the mouth.

Then tell him not to. Antony is different from other males. He won't lose control and start a frenzy.

How she wanted to believe that. *I'm not sure if we should go that far. I still don't know what he found out earlier, and we could be needed at any minute.*

Kai and Trina are watching Birkwood, and the others should be arriving soon as well. We can take an hour off.

As she eyed Antony, standing so close she could feel his heat, she teetered. It'd been a long time since she'd been naked with anyone. And while she wasn't embarrassed about nakedness, it would make her vulnerable. The most vulnerable she could be, apart from having Antony inside her as she orgasmed.

Antony gently brushed her cheek with his fingers, up to her forehead, and down the bridge of her nose. The light touch soothed her, and he murmured, "Don't feel pressured, Iris. Tell me to sod off, if you want. Not that I'm giving up, mind you. But I never want you to do something you don't want to do."

Her dragon said softly, *Let him in a little bit more. Have some fun. Be something other than a Protector.*

She'd been close to giving in, and her beast's words were a type of permission. So she laid a hand on Antony's chest and stroked, back and forth, loving how his breathing picked up and heart raced. "I want to see your body. Show me."

The corner of his mouth ticked up. "As you wish, my dear. But come. We need more space."

He took her hand, gently tugged her to the living room area, and gestured toward the sofa. "Sit down. Feel free to touch yourself, if you want. I won't mind."

She snorted. "You make it sound as if you're a professional stripper."

"You have no idea what I've had to do over the years. I once had to take off my clothes in front of a hen party. I ended up with far too many penis necklaces around my neck by the end."

As she gaped, he winked and moved a few feet away.

Her dragon spoke up. *Don't be jealous. Just sit down and enjoy.*

I'm NOT jealous.

You are. And that's okay. But I want to watch our male.

Iris didn't even argue with her beast. As soon as she sat down, Antony started humming some beat. She was about to ask what the bloody hell he was doing when he undid the first button on his shirt, and the next, and she forgot about everything but the skin he revealed.

By the time he finished the last one, she itched to caress the dark hair mixed with gray on his chest. His rather firm, defined chest, crisscrossed with a few faint scars.

Damn, he was sexy.

As he tossed away his shirt, revealing his upper half, he made an exaggerated flexing motion, as if he were a bodybuilder, complete with an expression that looked as if he were constipated.

Iris burst out laughing, and Antony grinned. "What?"

"You really don't want to know because it's not the least bit sexy."

"Now I'm curious." He stepped closer, squatted down, and put a hand to either side of her hips. Without his shirt, his heat and scent surrounded her. And she wanted to pull him close, feel his skin against hers, and do more than tease.

But she couldn't go all the way, couldn't risk a mate-claim frenzy. So she told the truth. "You looked like you needed to take a shite, is all."

He raised an eyebrow. "Whilst I was going for comedy, I try to avoid bathroom humor."

Her lips twitched. "Aye, I can't see you playing fart sounds with your hands and armpits."

He leaned in until his face was only a few inches from hers. "Is that what you want, Iris? Fart sounds?"

"Of course not. I heard more than enough of that during my time with the army. Men in their late teens and early twenties find bodily humor the funniest thing ever."

He chuckled. "Men of all ages, I'm afraid." He moved a hand to cup her cheek, and Iris leaned into his touch. "But all that matters to me is you laughed. And it's part of my new mission to make you do it as often as possible."

Her heart raced as his heated gaze never moved from hers. Some people said Iris could be intimidating, but Antony wasn't fooled.

Her dragon spoke up. *He understands us better than most.*

He frowned as he caressed her cheek with his thumb. "I hate those blasted contacts."

"I could take them out."

"Normally, yes, I'd say do it. However, in this moment, I like having you right where I want you."

"And where is that?"

His free hand moved to her upper thigh and stroked back and forth. Each pass made her heart pound and her pussy pulse. He whispered, "Wanting me."

She could make a quip, say he was cocky, and mention how their food was getting cold.

And yet, as he continued to stroke her thigh, she widened her legs more.

Antony chuckled as he moved closer, until he nearly touched her. He moved his head to her ear, nibbled her earlobe, and then said, "Let me take off your jeans and please you, Iris. Let me lick and nibble and make you squirm."

The pulsing between her thighs increased, and her breasts grew heavy. Before she could change her mind, she whispered, "Aye."

"Aye what?"

"Aye, do as you said."

"Then stand up, love. And let me help you out of those jeans. As much as I love how they highlight your arse and thighs, I want to see your beautiful skin."

He was smooth, almost too smooth. And yet, she heard nothing but truth in his voice.

Her dragon spoke up. *He fancies us. Don't second-guess it.*

For the first time in a long time, Iris embraced her emotions over her brain, and stood. She moved to undo her jeans, but Antony took her hands. After kissing the palm of each one, he released her and undid the button and zipper. He tugged, and she wiggled, and after a rather ungraceful dance, her jeans finally lay on the floor.

"Look at that little bow."

Damn, she'd forgotten about her underwear. "Just because I have a job mostly done by males doesn't mean I can't be girly with my underthings."

He traced the bow at the top of her underwear, back and forth, never quite touching her skin. "Of course you can. My boxers have little slices of pizza on them. Everyone is more than what we show to the world."

She blinked. "Pizza slices?"

He never took his gaze from the strip of skin between her top and her underwear. "That's a story for another time. I don't want to talk about my brother right now. I want to do this."

His lips brushed against her skin, and Iris's hands went to his head. As he did it again, the pounding between her legs increased, and she nearly pushed his head down.

As he spoke, his hot breath caressed her skin. "So warm and soft. I need to see more. Tell me I can."

Without hesitation, she whispered, "Aye."

Antony's patient movements vanished as he tugged down her underwear. As soon as she stepped out of them, he nuzzled the short hair at the apex of her thighs. She swore he said, "Mine," but before she could ask, he gently pushed her down and she plopped onto the couch.

His hand stroked her legs as he met her gaze. At the heat and desire there, her heart pounded.

"Open them for me, Iris. Let me see that pretty pussy of yours before I devour it."

Her dragon hummed. *Let him do that. I want to feel his mouth. Don't say no.*

At his look, Iris didn't think she could say no for anything, so she spread her legs.

Antony's fingers moved to her inner thighs, stroking back and forth, never quite reaching where she ached for him most. She growled. "Stop teasing me."

He ran a finger through her center, and she nearly moaned as he murmured, "So wet and ready for me, Iris. Normally, I'd be more patient. But I need to taste you, love. Say I can."

"Please, Antony. Hurry."

He nodded, pushed her legs wider, and lowered his head.

Antony had planned to draw out his first time with Iris. Bringing her close, backing off, and doing it again until she was sweaty and desperate and only then would he watch her fall apart and maybe even lower down her guard a little more.

But as he stared at her spread thighs, her pussy dripping for him, his legendary control snapped. After spreading her wide, he lowered his mouth and ran his tongue through her center. At the musky yet sweet taste, he groaned and his cock got even harder.

He lapped and nibbled and even fucked her with his tongue. However, he managed to hold back from teasing her clit. He sure as hell hoped this wasn't the only time with his dragonwoman, but he was determined to drink his fill of her sweet taste while he could.

Eventually, Iris dug her nails into his scalp and said, "Antony, please."

Lifting his head, he met her gaze, loving how her usual guard was down. Instead, she was a slightly disheveled woman with need burning in her dark brown eyes. For him. "Please, what? Tell me what you want, Iris, and it's yours."

She raised her hips. "I'm so close, Antony. Make me come."

Her words shot straight to his dick, and for a split second, he wanted to strip and take her right there on the sofa.

But he pushed down his own desires. He could have

more of this, he was certain of it, as long as he didn't fuck this up and rush things.

So he rubbed her thighs and settled back between her legs. "This flat is soundproofed, so scream for me, love. Let me know if you like it."

After running his tongue through her center, he flicked her hard little bud, and again, loving how she arched into his touch. He thrust a finger into her pussy as he suckled her clit. He swirled his tongue, and nibbled, and suckled again, until Iris finally broke apart. She cried out as her pussy squeezed and released his finger, over and over again. He drew it out, his mouth continuing to worship her, until Iris finally slumped and came down from her high.

Antony slowly raised his head, removed his finger, and licked it clean. Iris watched him, smiled, and then closed her eyes.

Needing to feel close to her, even if he couldn't be as close as he wanted, he crawled up beside her, pulled her body against his, and smiled as she snuggled into his side.

Seeing Iris naked from the waist down, her hair falling out of her ponytail, as she stroked his chest with her free hand, did something to his heart. It would be so easy to love this complicated woman, if he let himself.

Before he could think too much about it and all the dangers that came with it, Iris spoke. "I want to say something, but I know it'll make you cocky."

He kissed the top of her head and nearly crowed

when she didn't complain or scold him for it. "I can't be cocky if it's true. So let's hear it, love. What do you want to tell me?"

For a few beats, she merely stroked his chest, playing with his chest hair. Eventually, she replied, "Your mouth is good for more than talking."

He laughed. "Well, it's here to serve you whenever you wish, love."

For a second, he thought he'd fucked up. Iris hadn't committed to anything, might not want him as much as he wanted her. But then she snuggled more into his side, and he mentally breathed a sigh of relief.

She said, "I'll keep that in mind." Lifting her face to his, she added, "But what about you?"

His dick twitched at her words, but Antony did his best not to sound desperate or eager. "What about me?"

She arched an eyebrow. "Don't be obtuse. You're a clever male, aye? You know what I'm talking about."

"Aye, I do." She narrowed her eyes at his accent change, and he went back to his regular one. "I wasn't mocking you, I promise. It's called teasing."

Without another word, her hand went to his crotch and stroked his trousers over his cock. Antony sucked in a breath and barely heard her words as she said, "Two can play at that game."

As she gently squeezed, Antony moaned. "Tease me as much as you like, love. I want all of it."

Quicker than he thought she could, she'd undone his trousers and exposed his boxers. She snorted. "There really are pizza slices on your underwear. Is it to get me hungry before seeing your cock?"

"Hmm, does pizza make you starving and ready to eat some nice sausage?"

"Did you really just say that?"

He winked. "Yes, yes, I did."

She rolled her eyes, but her twitching lips made him keep going. "Just don't slice it into pieces for pizza. My brand of sausage is better eaten whole."

"It's a good thing you didn't go into comedy."

Unable to resist, he rolled until she was on her back on the couch with him nestled between her thighs. His dick throbbed in his boxers, but he did his best to focus on Iris and the moment. He wanted more than a quick fuck —he wanted a future. "I'm quite funny, I'll let you know."

"Says who?"

"I made you laugh."

She looked stern a second before she smiled and raised a hand to cup his cheek. "Aye, you did. I don't know why, but your bad jokes are somehow charming."

He ached to kiss her, to taste her lips and explore her mouth, but knew he couldn't. Not with a dragon-shifter. At least not with one who hadn't said yes to a possible mate-claim frenzy.

So Antony nuzzled her neck instead and lightly nibbled. "You taste fantastic."

One of her hands went to his back and lightly stroked. The slow motion, up and down, relaxed him.

She murmured, "I wish we could do this properly, Antony. But..."

"I know, we can't." He leaned back, searched her eyes, and said, "Not yet, at any rate. Maybe someday?"

She hesitated. Just as he was ready to say never mind, she nodded. "Aye, someday. I'd like that."

A thrill shot through him. "Good." *You're mine*, he didn't say.

Instead, he sat up, tugged Iris into his lap, and looped his arms around her waist. She moved to get more comfortable. Her arse brushed against his cock, and he groaned.

"Let me up, Antony. I'll return the favor and make you come, too."

He hugged her closer to him and laid his head over her heart. "Later. For now, I just want to hold you like this. I know it's so simple, and yet..."

"And yet, it's been a long time. Aye, it's the same for me, too."

He twisted his head a little to see her face. They stayed like that, his head on her chest and staring at one another, for nearly a minute before she bit her bottom lip. While she obviously debated something, he asked, "What is it?"

"I don't want to ruin the moment, aye?"

He tightened his arms around her waist. "When it's just you and me, ask or say anything, love. I mean it. We both have to be strong and controlled a lot of the time, hiding our true thoughts or opinions, and I don't want that here. Not between us."

She ran her nails through his hair, and he nearly hummed. "I'll try, but this is hard for me, aye? Sharing myself, my true self, isn't easy. Not even with my parents."

"Why not with them?"

She looked away. "My mum wanted a different future for me, a safer one. And whilst my dad was better, he worries as well. It was easier to share news about the lighter side of my job, the easy assignments, like with babysitting your brother. That kind of stuff."

"Babysitting Max for his public-facing persona. Yes, that is entirely accurate."

She smiled and met his gaze again. "When he lets down the act, he's a lot like you, in some respects. Which makes sense when..."

Her voice died down. "When, what?"

She shook her head. "I don't want to ruin our little bubble of peace and happiness."

Antony ignored the happiness part—which made him rather proud—and kept them on topic. "Tell me, Iris. I don't want there to be secrets between us."

As soon as he said the words, he mentally cursed. Iris required patience, not him saying they should bare all.

However, she didn't jerk back or try to get away. Instead, she traced his collarbone and blurted, "Max told me how you raised him after your parents died, but not much more than that. Such as how you managed it, after everything else."

Of course, Iris had figured out the timeline of his life. He yanked the blanket from the back of the sofa and spread it over his and Iris's lap. "There. Now you won't get cold."

Her gaze softened. "Thank you. Now, tell me."

As he debated what to say, she took one of his hands and threaded her fingers through his. He stared at their clasped fingers, and in that moment, Antony knew he would one day love this dragonwoman. And he needed to do everything he could to win her and not hold back because it might be painful someday.

And so he tightened his grip around her waist and debated where to start.

Chapter Eighteen

To most people, Antony would look almost nonchalant, with the corners of his mouth turning up slightly as if he were about to smile.

However, Iris could see the tenseness of his jaw, the way his eyes became a little distant, and she knew this was hard for him.

Aye, part of her still regretted bringing it up. And yet, the coming days would probably be crazy and busy and she might not have another chance to ask.

Her dragon spoke up. *You don't have to justify asking him. You're curious about him, just like me.*

Aye, but I still feel guilty about not making him orgasm like he did with us.

Later. We both want more than a onetime thing, aye? We need to be genuine.

Still, the longer Antony remained silent, the more

she started to think she should tease him or tickle him or distract him somehow. Then he tightened his hold on her waist and said, "I guess I should start by saying my parents weren't killed because of me or my job. No, it was a car accident. And yes, at first I thought maybe it was staged. However, it wasn't long before the drunk driver was arrested, confessed, and no amount of background checks by me or my colleagues found anything nefarious. Just an idiot, careless with other people's lives."

She squeezed his hand in hers. "I'm sorry."

He shook his head. "Don't be. The culprit died, in prison, of natural causes. It can't bring my parents back, but at least justice was served."

"Still, it's not easy, aye?"

"No. Although I haven't thought about it in years, to be honest. I was more concerned about Max being happy."

"How old was Max when your parents died?"

"He was just shy of fourteen. Not an easy age to begin with, but he ended up saving me, in a way. After Lisa's murder, I became obsessed with getting stronger and smarter and more clever about maneuvers. And at the time of the car crash, it'd been over a year since I'd visited my family. I didn't want to risk them getting hurt, too. Only once I was stronger could I see them. Then I didn't have a choice because there was no one else alive to take care of my brother.

"At first, I somewhat resented Max because it meant

I had a huge liability to look after. But once I saw him at our parents' funeral, looking lost and not his usual cheerful self, I realized how bloody selfish I was being. He was still a child, his whole world had tilted, and he needed me to step up. To better protect and look after him, I stepped away from the field and analyzed intelligence instead. Little did I know, my desk work would be extremely helpful later on.

"But back to Max—I had to be both brother and parent to him. It's when I started making jokes again, just to get him to smile. I encouraged his studies and interest in dragon-shifter history, especially archaeology. There was never a dragon-shifter version of *Time Team* —that old show where they had three days to investigate an archeological site and present their findings—but Max thought that maybe one day he could do it. Much like me, he was charming when needed and could make a good host. And I never laughed at the idea because once he fixated on something, he became somewhat obsessed, even if it got him into trouble."

Iris chuckled. "Aye, I could see him hosting a show. Whenever I had to take him to archaeological sites, Max often acted as a TV presenter, albeit a rambling one."

Antony smiled. "He might still do it one day, after he finishes with Dragon's Court."

"Maybe. Although given your caution and protectiveness, how did he end up working with you?"

He shrugged one shoulder. "Stubbornness runs in the family, and he built up this image of what I did and how he could save the world. The reality is a lot different, though. And since he has a softer heart than me, he couldn't live with the tough decisions he had to make."

She cupped his cheek, wanting to help ease the pain in his eyes. Pain she understood well herself. "Protecting people isn't always black and white, aye? Sometimes you have to make the difficult decision of who to save and who you can't."

"You've had to make that type of decision before, too?"

She nodded. "Aye. In the early days as a Protector, before Finn was in charge, the old leader wanted to attack the wee splinter clan, Seahaven, and force the dragon-shifters back to Lochguard."

Antony searched her eyes. "He wanted to start a war?"

"Aye. Toward the end, Dougal Munro became obsessed with online groups that pushed for dragon domination. He'd heard about Marcus King and Clan Skyhunter, and had even thought of reaching out to him, back before King changed tactics and started working with humans. Dougal thought that if Lochguard and Skyhunter banded together, they could surprise Stonefire and Snowridge and take them over. However, that kind of talk was too extreme for many, even for those who didn't like humans, and it's the reason why Lochguard voted to have a new clan leader trial." She tilted her head and studied Antony, noting how he wasn't surprised. "But you knew all of that already, didn't you?"

"Yes. I may, just may, have had an informant inside Lochguard, one who helped garner support for the new clan leader trial to challenge Dougal."

She should be angry. And yet, Iris had been privy to Dougal's ramblings, the ones the clan at large hadn't known about. Dougal hadn't been in his right mind at the end. "Your meddling might have saved Lochguard and prevented a dragon war. Finn has definitely been the better leader. But just how much meddling have you done over the years?"

"Well, I try to avoid meddling when possible, so very little. But Dougal Munro wanted to start a civil war, one that would've killed a lot of people, both human and dragon. It was a calculated choice."

Iris turned a little to better study Antony's face. "How did you stay in the shadows for so long? To the point we didn't know you existed?"

He gave a wry smile. "I was erased and invisible to the outside world for a long time. It was safer that way, especially as the government worked to better protect against hackers and cybersecurity threats. Having humans and dragon-shifters who didn't have any kind of records, like those on my team, meant our enemies wouldn't look for us."

"So what changed to bring you into the light again?"

He shrugged one shoulder. "Rosalind Abbott. When she took over the DDA, she was told about us and she reached out for a meeting. She convinced my superior that slowly having us in public, helping the dragon-shifters and humans alike, would make for better optics. Especially since Rosalind has plans she is determined to see through, ones that concern humans and dragons."

Iris had suspected for a long time that the DDA Director was playing 3D chess, always a few steps ahead of everyone else. "And you can't share any of those plans?"

He traced her cheek. "I'm afraid not, my dear. At least, not yet. Once we finish this business with the rogue dragon-shifters and your fellow Protectors, I'll be recruiting more people to work with my team. Ones I can share everything with. You, too, if you're still interested by the end."

Iris wanted to ask more about his proposal. However, at his mention of Zoe, guilt crashed over her. She needed to focus on helping her fellow clan member and changed the topic. "Speaking of Zoe and the others, you still need to tell me what you learned today."

"Back to work already." She arched an eyebrow, and he sighed. "Of course. But let's get cleaned up and sit down to eat, then I'll tell all."

As he helped her up off his lap, part of Iris wanted to hold Antony close and go back to cuddling on the sofa.

However, too many people were counting on her. Her wants and needs would have to wait.

Her dragon spoke up. *You act like we'll never be alone with Antony again.*

I hope we can be. But if we find the missing dragon-shifters and have to do a rescue mission, anything could happen. We've lost people before.

Don't think like that. Be positive, aye? Dad always says if you think you're defeated before you even start, it'll become reality.

I know, dragon. I know.

So Iris did her best to push her worries aside as she cleaned up, dressed, and brought the takeaway containers to the table. Once she and Antony were seated, she asked, "What did you learn?"

He grimaced, and her stomach dropped. This wasn't going to be good.

Antony wanted to keep Iris safe, and yet he couldn't keep things from her. That would be the fastest way to lose her.

So once she asked for the news, he took a deep breath and said, "I talked with Dr. Turner about the small object from the town today."

"So someone managed to retrieve it?"

"Yes, one of my people did, after I left, and they transported it down south to Dr. Turner. The object was a hollowed-out chestnut, filled with a tiny tube and release mechanism."

"A real one? How did they fit that in there? It's tiny."

"Yes, which means time and effort went into making

it. However, they made a mistake using a real chestnut because someone on Dr. Turner's team analyzed the shell down to its components, which tells us it came from a tree in South Ayrshire."

"Aye, I've heard of how certain amounts of elements or what have you can pinpoint a location, but Lochguard has never really had the ability. But does South Ayrshire mean anything?"

He nodded. "There's another abandoned castle there—Dalquharran Castle. One with a rumored set of secret tunnels."

She frowned. "That seems too easy and predictable to have the chestnut lead to a place with tunnels. Especially given how much we learned about the dragon hunters and their tunnels a few years ago. It might be a deliberate distraction or a trap."

"I agree. But the more worrying matter is what Dr. Turner thinks the gas used today will do. Namely, it can kill humans but only knocks out dragon-shifters."

"I've never heard of something working on both humans and dragon-shifters before, since our genetic makeup is a wee bit different. How did they do it?"

He shook his head. "I don't know. Dr. Turner and her team are still looking into it. However, our job became that much more important, given what someone might use this for—to destroy entire clans in one go."

Iris shook her head. "That doesn't make any sense. The dragon hunters in the past said their mission was to protect humans, at any cost. It's why they want dragon's blood—to heal everyone. No, they don't care about killing dragon-shifters in the process. But killing humans? That's a major shift, if true."

"I'm still trying to determine if that's their goal or not. However, I think the incident earlier today in the town was a test. They wanted to see if it would kill me and knock out whoever was watching me."

"So someone knows you're working with dragon-shifters?"

"I don't have any evidence yet, but my gut says yes. I'm waiting for MI5 and the DDA to respond and say what to do. All I know is that we're to keep investigating Birkwood Castle, and maybe Dalquharran Castle, and to be careful about it."

"Which means gas masks, and that won't allow us to be under the radar."

"Ah, but there is a way we can protect ourselves and still look like a normal person, going about their day."

"How?"

"One of my gadget treasures is a set of filters that go inside your nose and another set that attaches to your back teeth. They should keep us safe."

"Should?"

"Yes. It's not a guarantee. Max may back out because of it, not that I blame him. He has a daughter on the way and a mate to think of."

He studied Iris, wanting to say she needed to keep her distance until they knew the special filters worked.

However, doing that would push her away and

destroy any chance for a future with her. He had to let her do her job and trust she could protect herself.

Not that he liked it.

She's not like Lisa—she has years of special training. If she can survive, she will find a way.

Although his heart didn't like the logic, he willed himself to be the rational, level-headed leader he needed to be, not the man falling fast for a certain dragonwoman with lovely brown eyes.

So he asked, "So knowing all of this, do you still want to help with the search around Birkwood Castle?"

"You're not demanding I refuse and stay far away?"

"No. Even putting aside that I have more respect for you than that, you'd still find a way to scout the area if I said no. However, if you wish to work with Clan North-castle in Northern Ireland, on their latest lead about the dragon hunters, that option is also available. It's up to you."

And even though he'd lost his appetite, Antony forced himself to eat as he waited for Iris's answer. He wasn't entirely sure which option he wanted her to pick.

Iris knew Antony well enough now to recognize he wore his forced neutral expression. He wasn't trying to persuade her one way or the other. No, he trusted her to make the decision, knowing the risks, even if he might not want her near danger.

Her dragon spoke up. *As I told you, he's different.*

Even so, she'd still expected him to send her away at the first sign of danger. After all, it'd taken her a long time to convince the male dragon Protectors on Lochguard that she could handle herself.

And yet, with Antony, he'd listened to her frustrations and was giving her the choice. He may be clenching his jaw to keep his mouth shut, but the fact he didn't order her to flee at the first sign of danger did something to her heart.

Not wanting to focus on how the male was starting to mean something to her, she asked, "If the filters fail, has Dr. Turner found anything that will neutralize a minor exposure to this gas?"

"Not yet, but she's roped in Dr. Trahern Lewis and Dr. Emily Davies to help her."

Dr. Trahern Lewis was originally from the Welsh dragon clan but had moved to Stonefire a few years ago. "Isn't he newly mated, though?"

"Yes. I won't get into his personal life, as that's his business, but he seemed eager to bury himself in research. At any rate, they're working on it, but there's no guarantee."

"You want to tell me to stay away, aye?"

"Part of me does, yes. I would say the same to Max. However, both of you have minds of your own, and I'll respect your choices."

She tilted her head and studied the human. He was far more honest than most males she knew. Well, apart from a handful who were already mated, and she'd never fancied. Definitely nothing like what she felt for Antony.

A sliver of panic stabbed her heart. Was she making decisions based on him and not just her own goals?

How far would it go? Would he eventually dictate her life? After all, Iris had once trusted a male to respect her job and position, and that had ended in disaster.

Her dragon spoke up. *Stop comparing him to the ex-arsehole, and just talk with Antony. If you start building up walls again, I'll take control and tell him not to give up.*

She resisted smiling. *You would, too.*

Aye, of course. Now, talk with him. He can never replace me, but I wouldn't mind sharing with him.

I would never replace you, dragon. Ever.

I know. I am brilliant, aye?

She mentally chuckled, but finally replied to Antony, "I want to stay and help you and Max. However, you need to promise not to hover or make decisions based on just my safety and no one else's."

"I'll try my best, I promise. But when it comes to you and Max, I'm not sure if I can be as objective as I am with other members of my team." Before she could ask what he meant by that, Antony added, "Now, let's share what we each learned today and start adjusting our plans. Once the other teams arrive, I want to be able to debrief and finalize our search of the area."

"Have the others found anything?"

"I'm not sure yet. We deliberately compartmentalize. Regardless, we need to make sure there's nothing near Birkwood before moving elsewhere. I don't want to overlook something and learn later that Zoe and the others were here the whole time."

At the regret in his voice, Iris knew he'd had a few failures before. Ones that still haunted him.

She reached across the table, gently squeezed his arm, and released him. He smiled, she did the same, and then they discussed everything they'd learned that day.

As they shared information and strategies, Iris wondered if this could be her future—protecting her clan and her kind, all while still having someone to share her life with when she wasn't working.

She hoped more than she should that Antony was different. And while she wasn't going to shut him out to protect herself, if he betrayed her, she might just give up males entirely, no matter what her dragon wanted.

Chapter Nineteen

Dragonwomen had started to vanish.

Zoe had been keeping track of who she thought she could persuade to trust her. Every morning, she discreetly surveyed the cells around her, trying to determine who was in the mood to listen to her and maybe change their minds.

Then, one morning, someone was missing. The first female to disappear had been the one who cried all the time. She'd been separated from her son and worried about what had happened to him. She always pleaded with the guards, hoping they'd tell her where the boy was.

She'd been taken to be examined by a doctor and had never returned. The guards had used her disappearance to threaten the rest of them, saying that anyone else who acted up or became a problem would visit the doctor as well.

One other female had tested that theory, wanting any reason to heckle the human guards and spit on them. She'd also been taken away.

And now, days later, neither female had yet returned.

Some of the other prisoners had started to notice the disappearances as well, and rumors ran rampant. Most thought the females had been taken to be killed or impregnated. While their captors might eventually condition some of the females to follow orders and have them shift to draw dragon's blood, a better long-term strategy was to raise obedient dragon-shifter children and have them shift on demand. Which meant the impregnating route was more likely.

She resisted grimacing. The stories of some of the other facilities running experiments and getting dragonwomen pregnant still haunted her.

What she wouldn't give to worry about teenagers sneaking off of Lochguard again. It was miles better than trying to think like their enemy.

Her dragon would probably say something like it kept people safe. However, nothing but silence filled her mind.

How did humans endure the isolation?

Her cousin, Rebecca, sat down next to her. She'd been seeking out Zoe more and more often. And while she hadn't revealed all her secrets—Zoe thought she knew something important, probably learned from

Rebecca's father—she'd reminisced about their childhood.

Today, however, her cousin leaned closer to her ear and whispered, "A third one is missing."

"Aye. Her mouth probably got her in trouble."

Chelsea had been taunting the human guards more and more. Her plan was to get them frustrated, to the point they opened her cell and she could attack them and make a grand escape.

It was a stupid plan, given how the guards carried all kinds of dragon-specific weapons—special stun guns, tranquilizer dart guns, syringes, and more that Zoe hadn't been able to identify yet.

In the end, Chelsea had vomited for most of yesterday. By the time the guards had retrieved her, she'd barely been able to hold up her head.

Zoe hadn't eaten anything since.

Rebecca whispered so no one else could hear her. "I'm scared, Zoe."

She was just about to comfort her cousin when one of the guards opened the giant door at the end of the hallway and entered, with six other males behind him. He made a beeline for her cell.

Zoe stood and walked to the bars. Despite everything that had happened, she wanted to protect her cousin. Rebecca had started to see the light now that she was away from her domineering parents, and Zoe wanted to have both of them walk out of this place alive.

The male stopped in front of her. Like all the guards,

he wore a mask over his face and dark clothes. "That's her, the one planning to escape."

Before Zoe could think of what to do, there was a sharp pain in her neck, and the world faded away as she fell to the floor.

It'd taken nearly a week to assemble all of the other teams and outfit them with the discreet filters before they could search the hidden, underground areas of Birkwood Castle.

The days flew by as everyone shared information, devised plans, and waited for Dr. Turner's okay that the filters should keep them from dying, even if she couldn't guarantee it.

In the whirlwind, Iris hadn't spent much time alone with Antony. Certainly not enough to be intimate again, no matter how much she itched to see him fully naked.

Even now, as he gave some instructions to Kai Sutherland and Trina Lau, she stole a glance, loving how he talked with his hands and could make Kai roll his eyes at some corny joke.

Her dragon spoke up. *You love his jokes.*

Aye, maybe so, but I'm not going to encourage him.

So will you let him kiss us on the mouth once we finish this mission?

Maybe.

Even if the thought of being a mother scared her,

she'd seen how Faye MacKenzie balanced being a mum with being a Protector. It wasn't easy, but Faye's mate supported her. And the more Iris thought about it, the more she thought Antony would do the same. Not once had he tried to convince her to take a safer job, away from danger.

Her dragon spoke up again. *Then we need to watch his back and make sure he survives. I'm more than ready for sex and maybe a frenzy.*

The frenzy isn't guaranteed, dragon.

Maybe not. It's still unfair that male dragons can tell and females can't. Maybe Dr. Turner and Dr. Sid can come up with something so that female dragons can detect true mates, too.

She smiled. *I'll make sure to bring it up. Just don't expect them to drop everything, aye?*

A familiar voice filled her ear, and she shivered at the heat of his breath as Antony said, "Am I the reason for that gorgeous smile?"

She wanted to playfully push him, but had decided to be more professional around her fellow Protectors. She whispered back, low enough so none of the others could hear. "Wouldn't you like to know?"

He discreetly winked. "I'll get it out of you later."

Max's booming voice prevented her from replying. "Did you hear my question, Antony?"

"Yes. And no, you can't go off by yourself this time. You'll stay behind until we give you the green light. If we don't return, you know what to do."

Max crossed his arms over his chest. "I don't like it, but yes, I know—call my assigned contact in the DDA."

Alice sat a few seats down from Max and waved her hand. "I'm sitting right here, thank you very much. My name is Alice."

Before Max could reply, Antony jumped in. "Now, now, let's get along, shall we? We're due to leave within the hour and need to gear up. So, any last-minute questions about the plan?"

Gavin, the human male paired with Robin from Skyhunter, spoke up. "You're 100 percent sure that Dr. Turner's concoction will keep us from dying? I know every mission can be risky, but I don't want to rely on something and make plans around it, only to fail any of you."

Antony replied, "If it is the same type of gas, then yes, it will keep you from dying. The amount inhaled, however, depends on whether you'll fall into a coma or not. Your implanted tracker chip means we should be able to find you."

Gavin raised an eyebrow. "Should? I thought you said they were foolproof."

"To a point, but if the dragon hunters have spent the last few years devising new technologies and weapons, then we fight the unknown." He glanced around the room. "This is your last chance to back out of this mission and do perimeter surveillance instead." No one raised a hand. "Good. Then kit up and in fifty minutes we'll meet in the corridor just before the outer exit. Dismissed."

Everyone stood and headed toward their assigned temporary accommodations. Iris hung back with Antony until it was just them and Max. Only once the door shut from the others did Max speak again. "Don't do anything stupid, brother. I mean it."

"Likewise."

Max shook his head and then looked at Iris. "You, too. I might need a dragon guard for a secret dig coming up, and you're the only one I trust."

Iris smiled. "I'll keep that in mind."

With that, Max left. Antony turned toward her, took her hand and tugged her close. After he cupped her cheek, he murmured, "I know you're capable and could kick the arses of most of my team, but still be careful, okay? Once this is over, once we find the hidden female dragon-shifters, I want to go on holiday with you. Undress you slowly, make you scream again, and kiss you anywhere you would let me."

She looped her hands behind his neck and leaned against his hard chest. "I never thought I'd want to take a holiday, but I wouldn't mind some time with you. Alone. You naked in my bed is my current motivation to get this job done quickly."

He smiled. "Mine, too." After nuzzling her cheek, he whispered, "Stay safe, Iris. I'm selfish and want more time with you. A lot more."

"If you're selfish, then so am I. Despite your awful jokes."

Antony tickled her side, and she nearly yelped. He stopped and lightly swatted her bum. "You love them, you know it."

"Maybe."

He leaned back and searched her gaze, his expression unreadable. For once, she wished he wasn't so bloody good at keeping his thoughts private.

Her dragon spoke up. *Soon. Soon we can have him to ourselves and he'll let down his guard. You had better do it, too.*

Antony finally spoke again. "I want to say more, a lot more, but the clock is ticking. Let's get ready and find your clan member and the others so I can share more with you, love."

The "love" at the end of his sentence made her heart skip a beat. Somehow, this male had wormed his way past her walls. And maybe, just maybe, she never wanted him to leave.

But for the moment, she needed to focus on the assignment and finding Zoe. Only once she was safe could Iris be a little selfish and spend time with the male she fancied.

And so she nodded, and they went toward their separate temporary quarters to put on their gear and double-check they had Scarlett's backup inhaler medicine, the kind that would hopefully keep them from dying.

Chapter Twenty

I t wasn't long before Antony and Iris met up with the others and headed toward Birkwood Castle. Even though Antony should focus on what Max had discovered a few days ago—a hatch in the woods near the derelict building that led to a man-made tunnel —he kept thinking about his time alone with Iris and how he'd nearly spilled his feelings.

He regretted not telling her how much she meant to him already, how he wanted to know every little thing about her.

And for the first time in a long time, how she was his biggest weakness because if he lost her, he didn't know what he'd do. Probably spiral and seek out revenge, uncaring about his own life.

Stop thinking like that and focus. He needed a clear head and to not do anything stupid. How many times had he told his new recruits that, during training?

Maybe, just maybe, it was time for him to move to a job that was more behind the scenes than leading missions.

But that was something to sort out later. For the moment, he trekked through the forests near Birkwood Castle, under the faint moonlight, making as little noise as possible. Iris was behind him, and Kai and Trina a few feet further back. They'd all approach in a fan shape, just in case there were sentries. The scouting hadn't revealed any, but while Max had found one hatch into the tunnels, there was a good chance there were more.

As he approached the entrance, he halted and made the signal for Iris to do the same. Per the plan, they each placed the chain with a small inhaler around their neck, tucked under their protective vests, and then drew their stun guns. Antony had a pistol as well, but would only use it in extreme circumstances. He'd rather not kill if he could avoid it, and not just because of the amount of paperwork.

He waited for the other teams' flashes of light from small metal disks to signal they were ready. Once all five checked in, he glanced over at Iris. Even though she wore protective gear, including a close-fitting protective cap, she still made his heart skip a beat. She would be beautiful, no matter what she wore.

However, he packed away his feelings and desires. He wouldn't get anyone killed.

She nodded, and he returned the gesture. He flashed his own metal disk, catching the moonlight in a specific sequence, and counted to sixty. Once done, he waited as Joseph and Kaine from Northcastle approached the hatch. Joseph could unlock anything, and Kaine's hearing and sight would help keep his human partner safe.

He kept one eye on the pair and one on the surroundings. Only once Iris touched his arm—she could see far better in the dark and had agreed to signal success with two pats—did they slowly make their way toward the hatch. Kaine and Joseph would enter first, then Antony and Iris. After that, the others would approach in intervals. If there was an ambush, they needed to be prepared.

After stepping through the opening, which was about a foot shorter than him, Antony could just make out the walls and the floor, thanks to his special contacts. While not quite as good as night vision goggles, they were a vast improvement over regular human eyesight.

The walls were brick, as was the floor. However, a few were cracked and some of the mortar was missing. At first glance, he thought these tunnels had been here for decades.

Tucking that information away for later, he motioned for Iris to proceed him, so he could take up the rear.

The tunnel seemed to go on for miles, although he judged it to be only one before he spotted two doors— one at the very end and one to the right of it.

He and Iris stopped about a hundred feet behind

Joseph and Kaine, waiting for a signal that it was safe. Joseph carried a small heat detection device, which would let him know if there were any people behind the doors.

Eventually, he pointed to the one on the right and gave the signal for safe. Antony signed back for them to enter.

As soon as Joseph tested the door for traps, he opened it.

At the same time, the floor under him and Iris slid open, and they fell.

Within seconds, he hit the ground. But despite the pain he'd feel in the morning, he was alive. Antony rolled over and jumped up, only to find Iris was on her feet already. She gave the okay signal, and they both surveyed the space. It was dark, with a few faint lights flickering on the walls. However, he didn't see a door.

Which didn't mean there wasn't one, just that it was probably hidden.

Before he could signal Iris to help him look, a loud scraping sound filled the room. Turning, he saw a large opening and a second later, a small dragon, probably an older child's size, roared and barreled straight for Iris.

The space was too small for Iris to shift. And even though she jumped out of the way, the small dragon's tail swung and smacked her against the wall. The dragon roared again, foam dripping from its mouth as it stalked toward Iris's still form.

He refused to think the worst and focused. After

pulling out his stun gun, he shot a few barbs. And while they penetrated the scales and it went off, the dragon barely grunted.

The beast did, however, turn toward him.

The eyes were glowing, which wasn't normal. Add in the foaming mouth and one broken horn on its head, and the small dragon looked possessed.

He didn't waste time drawing his mini-tranquilizer gun. He fired, and again, but the small dragon didn't falter. No, it headed toward Antony.

From the corner of his eye, he saw Iris remained unconscious on the ground. In that second, he knew he had to get the dragon out of this room and back through the door.

But the only way to do that was to leave his dragonwoman.

Faint shouts from Joseph and Kaine overhead told him help was on the way, but since sound echoed in tunnels, he didn't know how long it'd take. He couldn't wait and hope someone would show up in time. Especially since the beast was gearing up to charge him.

If he was going to act, it was now or never.

So Antony walked backward, toward the door, and hit the dragon with another tranquilizer dart, hoping it would follow.

The beast roared and in the blink of an eye, it raced toward him, opened its mouth, and clamped its jaw up around his middle.

The dragon's teeth pierced his skin, pain shot

through Antony's body, and he screamed. Breathing became harder, and his vision began to swim.

As the small dragon raced out of the room, carrying him like a toy, Antony hoped his distraction had worked and that Iris was okay and would escape.

Then the world went black.

A scream jolted Iris awake, just in time to see the dragon carry Antony away in its mouth.

And he was limp.

She struggled to move, every nerve hurting. Her only thought was that she had to go after that mad dragon, had to help Antony.

And yet, she could barely crawl along the floor toward the door. The closer she got, the more blood she saw on the floor.

No, no, no. She wouldn't think of him dying. She couldn't.

Her dragon spoke up. *He's strong and resourceful. If there's a way to survive, Antony will find it. Now, pack away your emotions like in the army and help him.*

Her dragon's words snapped her back to the present. And while it was harder than any time in the past, she slowly pushed her panic and worry and fear down, deep down. The best way to help Antony was to remain calm and try to get up.

She stood slowly, ignoring the jolts of pain, and

studied the open door and hall in the distance. As far as she could tell, no one was there.

However, investigating the passageway alone would be stupid. She needed help, no matter how much she wanted to charge after Antony.

Just as she debated how to get out and ask for help, a rope dropped close to her, and Kai slid down it. As soon as his feet touched the ground, he surveyed the area as he said, "You're hurt. Where's Holbrook?"

After taking a deep breath to steady herself, she quickly explained what had happened and added, "We need to rescue him."

The door grunted as it slid closed inch by inch. Panic rushed through her—if it closed, she might not be able to get it open again. Antony might be lost forever.

Her training faded away as she tried to dart toward it, but Kai's arms wrapped around her middle and held her back. Struggling, she didn't even notice the pain. She blurted, "We can't just abandon him."

"Look at me, Iris." After a beat, she slowly turned her head until she complied. Kai continued, his voice firm but a wee bit softer, as he said, "We'll find him. But charging after a raging, unstable dragon will most likely get us all killed. We need to be clever about this, or we'll all die."

Her first instinct was to say Antony could already be dying. However, her dragon spoke up before she could spiral. *Antony is not only a valuable asset to the hunters, but also a fighter. If anyone can find a way to hang on and*

survive, *it's him. Let's be clever and not make things worse.*

But—

No buts. We'll find him, end of story.

Her beast's reassuring voice helped calm Iris a fraction. She'd watched emotions get others killed before. She needed to be strong, to be the bloody good tracker she knew she was, to find Antony and help him.

Not alone, though. She had some of the best Protectors in the country nearby, as well as Antony's team. Together, they could do this. She just knew it.

An unusual sense of calm came over her, and she stopped struggling. She said to Kai, "They'll probably keep him alive as long as they can get information out of him."

Although she knew Antony would rather die than share secrets.

Kai grunted. "I agree. Now, we need to retreat."

She wanted to shout no, she couldn't leave him behind. Even if she'd been unconscious, she knew Antony had garnered the dragon's attention to save her life.

Still, as she glanced at the blood trail on the ground —at Antony's blood—her throat tightened. Humans were so much more fragile than dragon-shifters. Had he survived?

He will. And we'll give him as much dragon's blood as needed to get him back to full health.

"Iris?"

She cleared her throat, nodded, and looked back at Kai. "Aye, we'll retreat. For now."

Especially since there could be listening devices anywhere. They'd been kitted out with mini-signal jammers, but she had no idea if they were still working.

Kai tied the end of the rope to make a sling seat, and Iris ignored her pride to sit on it. There was no way she could climb the rope unless her life was on the line.

And as they hauled her upward, she glanced at the now-closed door and the blood in front of it.

Right then and there, she vowed to rescue Antony, no matter what it took. Even if she eventually had to go in alone because of the danger, she would. Because he was her human, and she would finally claim him as hers, or die trying.

Chapter Twenty-One

As Zoe started regaining consciousness, she heard a hum of voices. Doing her best to remain still and not give herself away, the voices slowly became clearer until she could make them out.

A female said, "She's the perfect candidate—strong, young, and healthy. Surely this time the mind-control device will stick and not kill her."

A male voice replied, "She's a better information source than anything else. I still say torture her and learn what we can about Lochguard and the other dragon clans."

Another male voice jumped in. "But just think of the possibilities. Having the young dragon under our control already gave us *him*. Just imagine a full-grown beast doing our bidding. We could jumpstart the civil war sooner rather than later."

The female voice spoke again. "Let's finish the initial tests to better determine if her body will reject the implant or not. We only have two right now, and I don't want to waste one because we rushed. I'll be back in ten minutes."

The two male voices grew fainter until Zoe thought they were across a large room. This was her chance to survey her surroundings and make a plan.

Because she refused to be used as a guinea pig and possibly hurt her own clan members.

Cracking one eyelid open, she took a few seconds to adjust to the light. It was a large, open room full of small cages, beds, and various medical equipment and TV monitors.

She could just make out Chelsea unconscious in a bed, her body wrapped with some synthetic fabric, unmoving. The machines attached to her whirred and beeped at intervals. Another female, one she couldn't quite make out from this angle, lay on her side inside a cage. And at the far end of the room, Zoe spotted a young dragon asleep in an even bigger cage.

Ignoring the clenching of her heart—she could only imagine what they'd done to that young dragon—she searched the last part of the room and nearly gasped. Because lying on a bed, chained to railings, was the tall form of Antony Holbrook. Covered in bandages, he looked pale, far paler than she'd ever seen.

Did that mean someone was trying to rescue them and was nearby?

The thought gave Zoe strength and helped her mind to focus. She needed to find a way to escape, or at least signal to everyone else where she was. Because given what she knew of Antony and how important he was, someone would come looking for him.

She quickly took stock of her own situation—she was handcuffed to railings but otherwise wearing her normal clothes, without any kind of special restraints.

No doubt, they'd miscalculated the dosage of whatever drug they'd given her. Zoe's muscle mass was higher, given her job, than the other females. And it'd probably worn off sooner than it should have.

Which gave her a window, a narrow one, to overtake the two humans in this room, lock it down, and think of her next steps.

Ignoring how she wished she had her inner dragon, she counted the doors in the room—two. A smaller one the female had probably gone through, given the direction of her voice, and a larger one that could only be opened by some sort of computer or wireless remote.

If she could take out the males and block the smaller door, it should give her a little time. Aye, there might be something awful on the other side of the massive door. But she needed the chance to look at their computer system and try to signal her location. Thankfully, she'd taken some courses from Emma MacAllister—now Lamont—back when the female had offered it to the Protectors, so Zoe had a shot at disabling the security briefly.

The handcuffs weren't special and bent with a little force. Bit by bit, she stretched out one and then the other, careful to play sleeping whenever the males glanced in her direction. She kept an ear out for their conversation—revolving around getting a turn to impregnate a female dragon to help the cause—until she finally removed the cuffs.

Ignoring the urge to rub her wrists, she waited. While she didn't have long, she needed the two males to walk closer before she could knock them out cold.

Only then could she send a signal and hope someone was looking for them. Because not even the best Protector in the world could break out of this place on their own.

Hours later, Iris was finally cleared by Dr. Turner, albeit with strict instructions about what she could and couldn't do.

Not that Iris would follow them, if Antony needed her.

And even though Kai and the others had been sending her updates, she wanted to see for herself that Antony's tracking chip had blinked back on. It'd been shorting out, steadily moving south, until it settled in Glasgow. However, in the latest update, they still hadn't pinpointed his exact location. Although where they could hide him and who knew what else in a city of over

600,000 people, she had no idea. Especially since the Greater Glasgow area was nearly two million people, which was a far cry from the remoteness of Birkwood Castle.

She entered the room at the end of the hall—they were in yet another safe location for Antony's team—and walked in to see not only the tech she'd met in Inverness but also Arabella MacLeod, her clan leader's mate and one of the best hackers in the country. Both sat in front of a group of monitors, with various programs running in the background.

Arabella noticed her and motioned for her to come over. "I won't bother with small talk. We're about to pinpoint Antony's location, now that his tracking chip has remained on for more than a few minutes at a time."

"Where's Finn? Is he here?"

"No, he's back on Lochguard, watching the children and standing by in case he needs to contact the other clan leaders. Cooper, Faye, and Grant already have all the Protectors on standby."

Iris blinked. "Really?"

Arabella glanced up at her. "Of course. Not only to help Zoe, but also to find and rescue Antony. Given what Kai said, he risked his life to save yours. So we're not going to abandon him, if we can help it." Her pupils flashed to slits and back, and she continued, "Besides, he means something to you as well."

She blinked. "How do you..."

Arabella shrugged. "Being the clan leader's mate, you learn to watch out for the clan. And that male has helped you show a little more of yourself."

Had she been that transparent about her feelings?

Before she could reply, Robin from Skyhunter grunted. "I'm more concerned about Max's threats to give our clan hell if we don't save his brother."

Arabella raised a dark eyebrow. "Max is your problem, not ours. No, Iris has done a lot for Lochguard and it's time for us to help her in return."

For a second, Iris merely stared. She'd never been close to Arabella, but now she wondered if maybe she should've made more of an effort.

Her dragon spoke up. *We have time. I think maybe now you realize we shouldn't isolate so much from the clan and focus solely on work, aye?*

Before she could reply, a familiar female voice drifted from the doorway—it was Alice. "The DDA is willing to help, if it gets bad enough. Yes, the dragon hunters are a big pain in their backsides, but the thought of possessed dragons running around, snatching up people, scared the shit out of them." She stopped next to Iris. "Are you okay?"

For a split second, her steady facade faded, and her eyes heated with tears. She still didn't know if Antony was even alive.

But then Arabella spoke, and it helped her focus. "That can't be right."

Jessie Donovan

Iris asked, "What?"

Arabella frowned at the screen. "According to this, Antony is in Glasgow Central Station."

"The train station?"

Arabella nodded. "But surely not. If he'd escaped and made it there, someone would've called us by now."

The unnamed tech next to her nodded. "Yes, Antony could contact our boss within seconds, from any phone. So he must be there unwillingly, somehow."

Part of her wanted to ask who the bloody hell they worked for, but finding Antony was more important. "Then we need to go to Glasgow Central."

Arabella glanced at her. "You're in no state to be going anywhere."

"My ribs are already healing. I can help."

A voice boomed behind her—Kai Sutherland. "Iris, we'll find him. I vow it."

She turned toward the Stonefire head Protector. Truth radiated from his eyes. He added, "You've helped us before in the past, so let us do the same. Especially since you've helped protect Arabella over the years, and regardless of her mate, she's still one of ours."

Arabella was originally from Stonefire but had moved to Lochguard and eventually mated the clan leader. It'd helped to form the close bond between the two clans, arguably closer than between any other dragon clans in the UK, even if that was slowly changing.

Her dragon spoke up. *We need to trust him. Kai is a good male, and he will find Antony and Zoe.*

But it should be us.

Aye, maybe. But if it were another Protector, what would you tell them to do right now, if they were injured?

She mentally grumbled. *Their injury could do more damage than good.*

Aye. So let them find Antony. We need to give them the best chance at success.

Iris made a decision. "I'll stay back, out of danger, but I need to at least go to Glasgow, Ara. Please."

"As long as you let Kai and the others take the lead, I won't try to stop you. But just remember, Antony will need you when you find him. So don't do anything stupid."

"I won't." She glanced around the room. "Let's find out everything we can about Glasgow Central on the way."

Kai nodded. "This place is only about forty minutes away from Glasgow, and before we leave, I'll call in reinforcements. We'll have to drive, to keep a low profile. But those from Stonefire can fly most of the way and shouldn't be too far behind."

As everyone volunteered for tasks, Iris waited for regret or doubt to rush in about not having a lead role this time.

But it never came.

Sharing responsibilities didn't make her a failure. If

anything, she now had multiple people capable of stepping in and getting the job done.

And so Iris formed a plan with everyone else, and was soon on the way to Glasgow, hoping they would get there before it was too late.

Chapter Twenty-Two

During the drive, they'd learned that Glasgow Central Station had old passageways and platforms beneath it, creating a labyrinth mostly unavailable to the public.

Joseph Doyle had reached out to some of his contacts to ensure the underground tours were cancelled for the day. While unlikely they'd have to explore any areas used by the tour guide, they didn't want to chance it.

Now, she was walking with her assigned partner to one of the old underground entrances, kept secret from almost everyone in case it was needed during an attack or war. Antony's department and MI5 were the only ones who knew the location. At least, until today.

She wondered just how many secrets Antony protected. Once she found him—because she would—she'd make sure he promised not to keep any from her.

Max walked next to her—he'd somehow talked the others into allowing him to accompany and hang back with Iris—and asked quietly, "You're quite sure you're not claustrophobic?"

She resisted rolling her eyes. "I told you, no."

"Just making sure. Until my brother is back and well, it's my job to look after you."

She glanced at Max, noticing how serious he was. "I appreciate it, but I'm fine, aye? The ride down did wonders, and my ribs are as good as new."

"You may be physically fine, but there are other ways to hurt."

"You're more astute than I thought, aye?"

He winked. "You're getting to know the real me. Just try not to fall in love with me, because Lavinia won't like it. She's quite possessive, and rightly so."

She huffed a laugh. "I'll do my best, I promise."

They reached the address where a secret basement door led to the underground passageways. However, they went to the front door, knocked, and were let inside. Killian O'Shea and Kerry Penrose stood to the side, waiting for them.

Iris didn't want bodyguards, but they'd agreed working in teams would be best.

The female dragon, Kerry, smiled at Max. "Too bad you're mated. You're definitely the better looking brother."

Iris growled, but Max merely bowed at Kerry. "Alas, I am mated. You'll just have to resist me."

Killian grunted. "Enough. If we don't want to get too far behind, we need to go."

Each team had been assigned different sections to explore. Iris argued and persuaded everyone that she could look at the areas closest to the entrance. She nudged Max. "Come on, or I might tell Lavinia you're flirting whilst she's back home, pregnant and digging in the dirt."

He narrowed his eyes briefly—so briefly only Iris would notice—before falling back into his easy-going persona. "Tut, tut, we can't have that, can we? Lavinia is the moon and stars, my empress and queen."

Killian turned without another word and headed downstairs, followed by Kerry, and then Iris and Max. They arrived at a door guarded by Nikki Gray-Hartley and Rafe Hartley, a mated dragon-human pair from Stonefire. Nikki was a Protector, and Rafe was human and an army liaison with the dragon-shifters.

It didn't escape her notice that a human and dragon guard team would have a better chance at surviving some sort of chemical attack.

Although Iris hoped nothing would happen. Nikki was brilliant at her job, and they'd banded together a few times during the intra-clan meetings on Stonefire and Lochguard.

Her dragon spoke up. *Nikki knows what she's doing. And for a human, Rafe is okay.*

She mentally snorted. *Rafe is more than merely okay, dragon.*

Maybe. If you like the muscled, scowling type.

Suppressing a smile at her beast, Iris followed the others through the door and down the stairs, down some more, and yet some more, until they were pretty far below street level. They exited onto an abandoned platform from Victorian times, and Killian motioned for Iris and Max to wait while he and Kerry scouted ahead.

Iris surveyed the space, noting a few old doorways to what must've been maintenance rooms, when Kerry's voice shouted, "Gavin? What are you doing?"

A scream followed. Iris dashed down the old tunnel Killian and Kerry had used, pulling out her tranquilizer gun as she ran. Another scream was cut short, followed by some grunting.

Iris entered a larger space where two sets of tracks could be laid side-by-side. Kerry was unconscious on the floor, and Killian battled against a number of humans. One who looked just like Gavin Edwards from Antony's team.

But as he attacked with his left hand, something wasn't right.

Then it hit her—he looked like Gavin, but wasn't him. The real Gavin was right-handed and had a wee freckle on his neck, which this male didn't.

Scanning the area, she calculated that she and Killian were outnumbered three to one. The only way to win would be if they could toss a gas canister to render the humans unconscious. Iris, Max, and the others on her side wore the discreet filters and should be safe.

Max caught up to her, and an idea flashed from a memory. Long ago, before she'd learned the truth about Max, he'd grumbled about a dig having to be halted for a day since someone got heat stroke and fainted. He'd gone on and on about everyone rushing to help, nearly ruining their grid lines, and other details she'd blocked out.

Like someone fainting from heat stroke, she needed something big to garner their attention, just long enough to incapacitate them.

Leaning to Max, she handed him the canister. "Pull the ring at the right moment."

She imagined wings sprouting from her back. They grew and grew, brushing the sides of the large room. It was a tight fit, but she just managed to flap them. The force of the wind knocked a few people down.

Just as a bullet pierced her wing, Max pulled the ring and tossed the canister.

Iris knelt down, hoping she wouldn't do irrevocable damage as she imagined her wing merging into her body. Once complete, pain shot through her and she could feel blood dripping down her back.

However, as the gas slowly knocked the humans out, Killian and Max went to help Kerry and then used Killian's zip ties to bind all the humans.

The pain in Iris's back dulled, and she knew it wasn't life-threatening. Although she hoped her wing would heal properly despite shifting while injured, which was a big no-no for any dragon-shifter.

Pushing that aside, she struggled to her feet and went to Killian, Max, and Kerry—who was awake again —and stood next to them. Kerry spoke first. "That's not Gavin, but it looks just like him."

"A twin, maybe? Or a family member."

Kerry replied bitterly, "One he probably told everything to. I can't believe I ever fancied him."

Killian grunted. "You don't know for sure he did. At any rate, backup should be here any second—"

Before he finished, a mixture of humans and Protectors flooded the room. After quickly debriefing them, everyone went to work carting the unconscious humans off.

Alice walked over to them and nodded. "The DDA will take care of these people for now. Contact me whenever you've finished your mission and we'll talk."

The female walked off before anyone could say a word.

Iris was about to ask Killian if they should keep searching down this tunnel when the wall off to the side began to open and a blaring sound filled the space.

She braced herself, wondering what the bloody hell was happening now.

Zoe struggled to keep her breathing slow and even as the two males approached her. The female would be back at any minute, and once she returned, Zoe's chance of signaling to the others where she was would be zero.

Once they were close enough, she sprung up and jumped over them, twisting, to land on her feet. She didn't waste time, bashing their heads together hard enough to knock them unconscious without killing them.

Even though her head still pounded from whatever drugs they'd given her, she pushed it aside and dashed to the main computer terminal. The small dragon lifted his head and stared at her, but she ignored him for now. After all, she couldn't help the wee male unless her clan could find them.

The computers weren't locked or password protected—highlighting the arrogance of whoever was in charge—and Zoe searched for any sort of remote control panel or security system.

Bingo, she found it within seconds. As she'd thought, she could lock the doors from inside. Just in time, too, because someone started to pound on the smaller door, probably the human female.

Zoe ignored the noise, looking for either a way to broadcast her location or to open the giant set of doors.

Sirens blared just as she tried something to open the large doors. They slid apart slowly, and a cloud of smoke or gas or something rushed into the room. Zoe coughed and did her best to cover her mouth. However, while it tickled her throat, it didn't make her woozy or fall unconscious.

In fact, the young dragon was fine as well.

Then the smaller door finally burst inward, and some humans rushed inside. Before she could try leaving through the bigger door to get help for the others, the humans coughed and soon dropped like flies.

However, she didn't spot the human female among them.

Just as she debated securing the humans or going for help, Killian O'Shea rushed inside, followed soon after by Iris, Max Holbrook, and a female dragon-shifter she didn't know.

They had been looking for her. She'd just known it.

She should be thrilled. And yet, her dragon was still silent.

Focus on getting everyone to safety. Dr. McFarland and the other doctors can help you then.

So Zoe went to meet Iris, and the scent of blood hit her nose. "Iris, are you okay?"

"I'm well enough for now. Is..."

That's when Iris's gaze fell on Antony Holbrook. Zoe said, "Aye, he's here. But I don't know much about his condition, except that he's alive."

Iris nodded as worry flashed across her gaze. Then she rushed over to the human.

Something had happened in the time since Iris had left Lochguard. And as she watched Iris gently touching Antony's face, she smiled. It was about time Iris let someone in.

But thinking about someone letting her in again, she thought about her cousin. Despite their problems, she didn't want to leave Rebecca in the hands of dragon hunters, or whoever held them. Especially since there was a chance, a wee one, that she could help her cousin accept humans and come back to Lochguard.

And so Zoe went to Killian and the others to share everything she knew and see if they could help find and free the remaining dragon-shifter prisoners.

Chapter Twenty-Three

Antony's head pounded as he slowly woke up to beeping. It was rhythmic, just like a heart rate monitor in a hospital.

His body also throbbed, especially around the middle. Then he remembered—a dragon had carted him off, as if he'd been a piece of meat.

But at least the pain meant he was still alive. Next was trying to determine where he was and form a plan.

So even though his eyelids felt like concrete blocks, little by little he opened them, until he blinked against the dim lighting in the room.

Decades of habit meant scanning the space. However, once he saw Iris slumped over on his bed, her head cradled in her arms, he mustered the strength to lift his hand and touch her cheek.

She jerked awake, standing and looking around the

room as she blinked the weariness away. The sight of her disheveled and sleepy made him smile. His voice was scratchy as he said, "This wasn't how I wanted to wake up next to you for the first time, but I'll take it."

Her gaze shot to his, and she sat down and placed her hand over his. "Antony, you're awake! And strong enough to make pithy comments, so I'll take that as a good sign."

For a few seconds, he stared into Iris's lovely brown eyes. The flashes of relief and happiness did something to his heart. "I thought I would never see you again."

"Aye, and if you weren't still healing, I'd punch your arm. What were you thinking, distracting an unstable, mad dragon? He could've killed you, Antony. When I saw all that blood..."

Her voice cracked, and he brought her hand to his mouth to kiss the back of it. "I'm sorry, love. I couldn't stand by and watch him kill the woman I love."

For a second, he mentally cursed. Iris required patience, and he'd just gone and blurted out his feelings.

But instead of stiffening and making some dismissive comment, she cupped his cheek. As she stroked her thumb, he nearly purred. She said softly, "I've been trying to deny things, too afraid you'd betray me like my ex. But you were willing to die for me, Antony Holbrook. And when I thought I might never see you again? It made me realize how far you've burrowed through my walls, and I don't want to patch them up again. I love you, too. But just remember, I can shift into a dragon. So make sure not to charm too many females whilst doing a job."

At her words, his heart soared, and he wished he could kiss her.

But even putting aside how he probably couldn't quite sit upright by himself yet, there was the whole possibility of a mate-claim frenzy.

The thought of him and Iris having a child together someday made his earlier decision all the easier to share. "That won't be a problem, love. I've been too stubborn for years, and nearly being eaten by a dragon only made it all the more clearer that I need to retire from leading in the field."

Her brows came together. "Are you sure? It's been your life for over twenty years."

He gripped her hand tighter in his. "Yes, I'm sure. There's a lot I can do from behind-the-scenes." He hesitated, but didn't want to ever hold back with Iris. So he added, "Besides, if we kiss and there's a mate-claim frenzy, it means I can stay home with the baby whilst you continue working."

She didn't bat an eyelash as she replied, "I have a hard time imagining you as a stay-at-home dad."

"Well, I can work when the baby naps. I am the king of surviving on little sleep and multitasking."

"We don't even know if there will be a frenzy, aye? So let's not count our chickens before they hatch."

He studied her a second before stating, "Would you

be all right with a frenzy, Iris? If not, I'm sure Dr. Turner can think of a way to suppress it. She often goes on about how ridiculous it is that if she kisses some stranger, then she doesn't get a choice in whether she wants to have a child or not, unless she wants to drug her inner dragon for months."

He rather agreed with her. But he'd find ways to fund her research more later. Right now, he held his breath as he waited for Iris's answer.

After searching his gaze for a few seconds, she replied, "I'm open to it on three conditions."

His lips twitched. "Go ahead, my dear. What are they?"

"First, I want to work with you and your Wicked Security team, department, whatever it is."

"Of course. That one's easy."

She blinked. "It is?"

"Yes. That was my plan all along, remember?"

"Aye, well, I wasn't sure after everything that happened. And it was a sort of test, to show you were sincere about me doing the type of job I love, despite the possible dangers."

"I may not always like where you go or who you have to fight. But I also know asking you to give it up would make you slowly die inside. Besides, I love you exactly as you are, Iris Mahajan. Apart from maybe laughing at my jokes more often, I wouldn't change a thing."

She smiled and rolled her eyes. "Your jokes are occasionally funny."

He grinned. "I knew it! You're a die-hard Antony Holbrook fan."

"Let's not get too crazy, aye?"

"And the other conditions?"

She shrugged one shoulder. "Well, the second is that I still want to spend most of our time on Lochguard. Aye, we can visit Max and Lavinia on Skyhunter, but I don't want to leave my parents."

"Oh lord, your parents. You're going to have to tell me how to charm them."

She snorted. "My mum will be happy I've found a male at all. My dad, though, will probably quiz you and maybe challenge you to some inane contest with snooker or cricket or some other sport I never really cared about, but he loves."

"I'm quite good at cricket, especially bowling. So winning over your father should be easy. And yes, we can mostly live on Lochguard. Whilst my dragon-shifter team members have their own secret living arrangements, us living there might jeopardize them all if we have to visit Lochguard often. The more comings and goings, the more chance of discovery, after all."

"All these secrets of yours are going to take a lifetime to unravel, aye?"

He squeezed her hand. "I'll try my best, love. Although I'd rather focus on our story for most of it instead of the past. After all, we're just getting started."

She traced his jaw as her pupils flashed. "Sometimes, I still can't believe this isn't all an act and I'll wake up to find you walking away."

"Iris, listen to me. If I were healthy again, I'd pull you close and tell you in no uncertain terms that I'm here to stay. Once a Holbrook makes a decision, we stick to it." He tried to scoot over, and pain shot through his side.

"Stop that right now, Antony. You'll hurt yourself again, and giving you my dragon's blood will be all for nothing."

"Ah, that must be why I'm not in complete agony. Your blood must be as sweet as every other part of you."

He winked, and she sighed. "Oh no, there's going to be a lifetime of this, isn't there?"

"Yes, love. And it'll be a grand time, too. Well, I think so. There's still one more condition you haven't shared with me yet."

"You never miss anything, do you?"

"Not often. I'm sure you'll let me know when I do. Now, what's your remaining condition?"

She picked at the sheets of his bed. "Whilst I do want a frenzy at some point, after you're well, I want our first kiss to happen naturally and not be forced."

"Are you asking me out on a date?"

"Aye, maybe."

"Maybe isn't good enough, love."

"If you think I'm going to spout off nonsense like you would, then you'll be waiting a long time."

He chuckled, uncaring that it sent a dull ache

through his side. "Of course I don't want our first proper kiss to be forced, Iris. We have time to discuss future plans, though, since I don't know how long I'll be here."

The machines and room said he was at the secret research facility near London.

"Dr. Turner, Dr. McFarland, and Dr. Sid are all here, working together. And no, not just for you, either. They're trying to help the young dragon found in the same room as you, as well as the dragon female named Chelsea. The other female dragon we found died shortly after the rescue from some experimental brain surgery those monsters had conducted on her. The doctors are trying to figure out what they'd attempted—something to do with mind control, according to Zoe—to better prepare for the future. Because over the last few years, everything points to the dragon hunters researching ways to kill or control dragon-shifters."

Before he could ask for specifics, Iris filled him in on everything that had happened since they'd found him.

Apparently, he'd been in a secret research facility underneath Glasgow Central Station. The ones running it were an offshoot of the dragon hunters, although no one had revealed who was in charge. Zoe Watson had said it was a human female, probably Margot Green, but they had yet to confirm it.

The location of the missing dragon-shifters had been in the computer system back in the secret lab in Glasgow. The rescue teams had arrived just after the gas had gone off in the cells—probably a last-ditch tactic to prevent any witnesses—and they'd managed to save most of the prisoners, thanks to Dr. Turner's research, with help from Dr. Trahern Lewis.

The DDA was interrogating everyone they could, and soon some dragon-shifters would get the chance, too.

By the end, Antony's head throbbed from trying to keep everything straight. Which was bloody frustrating since he usually kept twenty different lists going at once without blinking.

He muttered, "I hate being weak and confined to this bed."

Iris raised her brows. "If you even think of trying to sneak out and start analyzing data before the doctors give you the all clear, I will tie you to that bed, Antony Holbrook. Don't think I won't."

"I never knew you fancied tying me up, Iris. Maybe we'll try that sometime." But his teasing didn't budge her stubborn expression, and he sighed. "Fine, fine, I'll be a good lad. But only if you come here and take a nap with me."

She eyed the empty space he'd created earlier. "I don't want to hurt you."

"You won't. Now, come here, love. Give your man some cuddles."

Chuckling, she laid down next to him carefully, and Antony slowly wrapped an arm around her. He didn't even grunt at the pain, loving how it felt to have Iris with him again. Especially since he hadn't been sure he would survive the dragon carrying him off.

As he breathed in her scent, a sense of peace and happiness settled over him.

And before he could tease her further, her heat and closeness lulled him to sleep, where he had dreams of mating her in front of her clan and making the dragonwoman his forever.

Chapter Twenty-Four

The next month flew by for Iris. Between visiting Antony, helping the other Protectors and Wicked security team members question the dragon prisoners, and staying in the loop with the DDA, she barely had time to eat and let her dragon fly for a bit each day.

However, as Antony's team shared more responsibility with her, she earned their trust bit by bit.

The hardest part had been keeping Antony from leaving his hospital bed too soon. However, his stubbornness and crankiness weren't any worse than a dragon-shifter male, and the doctors had handled him deftly.

But today was the day he would finally arrive on Lochguard. Iris had come home ahead to get everything ready for him. Unfortunately, that meant her mother sat right next to her as they waited for Antony to arrive at Lochguard's Protector building.

Iris glanced at her mother, who was knitting something for Antony that looked to be like a jumper with a dragon on it. A purple dragon, which was the color of Iris's.

Her inner beast spoke up. *I can't wait to see him wear it.*

I might burn it before that happens.

Oh, come on. It'll be fun to see the put-together, charismatic secret agent in a homemade dragon jumper. Maybe we should suggest she knit wings on the back, too.

Don't even think about it.

Her dragon sniffed. *You're no fun.*

Her mum's voice prevented Iris from replying. "I won't stay long, like I promised. But I need to meet my future son-in-law before the rest of the clan."

"I told you, we haven't discussed mating yet. So don't bring it up, aye?"

Her mother glanced at her before looking back at her needles. "Even Finn speaks well of him. He'll stay, I think. And mate you, too."

"Just because you say it doesn't make it true."

"Maybe. But you want him—both to stay and mate you—so I'm going to wish with my whole heart for it to become reality."

Sometimes she forgot how perceptive her mother could be. "Thank you, Mum. I do love him, but it's still early days."

"Don't worry, if he hurts you, I'll get the sons of my friends to teach him a lesson."

"Mu-um, no!"

Her mother smiled. "You are so easy to rile, Iris. I'll wait until after I know him a bit better before I ask my friends' sons. But it's always an option."

As Iris tried to think of how to dissuade her mother— telling her to stop would probably make her dig in—there was a knock on the door and Cooper walked in, with Antony right behind him.

Everything faded away as her eyes met Antony's. He winked at her, and she stood and rushed over to him. He engulfed her in a hug, and uncaring about the others watching, she merely listened to his heartbeat as his presence eased her tension away.

Her dragon spoke up. *We should definitely mate him.*

Cooper cleared his throat, and Iris raised her head. Her friend smiled. "I'll leave you to it, then. And don't worry, I'll take over your liaison duties with the DDA for as long as you need. Spend some time with your male."

With that, Cooper left, and Iris took a deep breath. Because now she would have to deal with her mother.

Stepping back, she turned and gestured toward Antony. He immediately took her hand as she said, "Mum, this is Antony Holbrook. Antony, this is my mother, Jhanvi Mahajan."

Her mother put down her knitting and studied Antony. He bowed and said, "Delighted to meet you, Mrs. Mahajan."

Jessie Donovan

Her mother snorted. "Iris said you were a charmer. Come here, son, and let me get a good look at you."

Antony gave Iris an amused glance before going over to her mother. Jhanvi was short for a dragon-shifter, at about five-foot-nine, making her quite a bit shorter than Antony. And yet, she wasted no time taking out a tape measure and wrapping it around Antony's chest.

"I need to make sure the jumper I'm making you will fit. Now, stand still."

Iris bit her lip to keep from laughing as her mother measured Antony's chest, arms, neck, and waist. The whole time he attempted to look stony-faced, except his lips twitched every now and then.

Once her mother finished, she stepped back and nodded. "For a human, you're a nice, strong male. Good. Let's hope that means you'll give me strong grandchildren, too."

Antony quirked an eyebrow as Iris groaned and then said, "Mother, stop. You promised."

Her mother waved a hand in dismissal. "Your father is getting on in years, Iris. I don't have time to beat around the bush." After patting Antony's arm, her mother gathered her stuff and said, "Make sure he comes to dinner tonight. Your father wants a turn to question him, although I think he'll do, as the Scots like to say."

Before she could think of how to reply to that, her mother left. As soon as the door clicked closed, Antony chuckled, came over to her, and hugged her close. After kissing the top of her head, he said, "I like her."

Iris laid her forehead against his chest and shook her head. "Please don't encourage her, aye? Otherwise, it'll only get worse."

He tightened his arms around her. "I assure you, I can handle your mother. Former secret spy, remember?"

She lifted her head and met his gaze again. "You say that, but you clearly underestimate my mother's ability to observe or guilt-trip or quietly manipulate things to the way she likes. Not in an evil way, but still."

"Then I look forward to the challenge. Maybe I should recruit her for Wicked security..."

"Don't you even dare!"

He laughed. "I won't, I promise. Now, how about you show us to our new home?"

Iris had been the one to suggest Antony stay with her. However, her heart still pounded as she led him out of the Protector building.

Her dragon spoke up. *It'll be fine. There's always the extra bedroom, in case you need to kick him out of our room for a bit.*

Antony's voice prevented her from replying to her beast. "If you've changed your mind, Iris, that's fine. I hear there are some young dragonmen with a spare room these days. MacAllister brothers, I believe."

"How in the world do you know about Ian, Connor, and Jamie MacAllister needing a roommate?"

"Spy mastermind, remember?"

She rolled her eyes. "We're going to have to set some

rules going forward, aye? Lochguard is to be our home, so no spying, unless you think there's a threat."

He sobered. "I know, love. I learned about the MacAllister brothers after working with Emma and Logan. Logan moved out, and well, no one has moved in with them since."

She softened. "Sorry. My mum put me on edge today. And whilst I'm glad she seems to approve, you still haven't met my dad yet. Or, the rest of the clan."

He took her hand, threaded his fingers through hers, and brought it to his mouth to kiss the back of her hand. The brief contact sent a little thrill through her.

Her dragon spoke up. *We should skip dinner and eat alone with Antony. Maybe he'll kiss us.*

Soon, dragon. When it happens, it happens. I'm not planning anything.

Her beast sniffed. *Well, I hope it happens before dinner, aye? I want him.*

Antony squeezed her hand in his. "Is your dragon saying good things about me? About how handsome and strong and clever I am?"

She snorted. "Wouldn't you like to know?"

He tugged her off to the side, behind a tree, and gently pinned her against it. His hard, lean body against hers made her heart race and lips ache to kiss him. He lowered his head, nuzzled her cheek, and said, "I think she's remembering my little strip show for you, love, and what happened after. Even now, I crave your taste and heat and the little sounds of your moans."

His words shot straight between her thighs. "Antony."

"I love the way you say my name, Iris." He raised a hand to fondle her breast, and Iris arched into his touch. "I'm curious how it'll sound when you come apart whilst I'm inside you."

Her dragon hummed. *Kiss him. Now.*

Not until we're somewhere private.

Then hurry!

Iris took Antony's face in her hands and stroked his cheeks with her thumbs, loving the late-day stubble against her skin. "I want to kiss you, but not here. Last chance—are you willing to risk a mate-claim frenzy?"

"I'm ready, if you are."

"Aye. Now, come on."

She pushed against his chest. He stepped back, and Iris took his hand before nearly jogging down the pathway to her house.

Maybe she should wait until later, allowing Antony time to settle in, but seeing him again, holding him, and him interacting with her mother, made Iris want to kiss and finally claim him.

And if there was a mate-claim frenzy and a child? She was okay with that because Antony wouldn't abandon her.

So she hurried the male she loved toward her cottage, eager to do something for herself and not for the clan. While she loved her job, wouldn't have any other, she was done burying herself in work and hiding from life.

It was high time to embrace it, starting with Antony Holbrook.

Chapter Twenty-Five

Antony hadn't planned to move so quickly, but he'd burned to kiss Iris and been more than happy to follow her through the clan. She'd even taken the least populated route, judging by the lack of people, and she tugged him inside a little stone cottage.

Before he could say a word, she went down the hallway and into a room that turned out to be a bedroom. He barely noticed the blue walls and shelf of knickknacks before Iris released his hand and ran it up his chest, to his neck, until she lightly caressed his skin.

Blood shot straight to his cock, and with a growl, he gently took Iris's face between his hands. "Tell me I can kiss you, love. I'm burning to feel your lips, learn your taste, and make you moan."

Her pupils flashed to slits and back before she

smiled at him. Even though she smiled more and more often these days, he treasured every one she gave.

Leaning against him, she murmured, "Kiss me, Antony. Please."

His self-control snapped, and he took her lips in a fierce yet gentle kiss. She was so soft, so warm, and he wanted more. So much more.

And yet, he needed to know if there would be a frenzy or not. So, drawing on every bit of self-control he possessed, Antony pulled back to find Iris's pupils flashing rapidly. "Iris?"

She growled. "My dragon is threatening to take control if you don't claim me. And soon."

A thrill shot through him. "I'm your true mate?"

She nodded, clearly struggling to keep her dragon in check. "Aye. Now, claim me, Antony. I want the first time to be with me and not my dragon."

"I will. But I want you naked first." He tugged at her top, and she raised her arms. Once the top was off, he turned her around to unhook her bra. That's when he saw the large, ugly scar on her back. He traced the shape as he asked, "Was this from when your wing was shot?"

She growled. "You want to ask about that now?"

He resisted chuckling. Instead, he knew that if he threaded a little dominance into his voice, her dragon should behave for a short while. So he stated, "Yes. Tell me what happened, Iris. I need to know if you're still hurting."

After a beat, she replied, "Aye, it's from my wing

wound, but it doesn't hurt anymore. I'll always have the scar, though."

Leaning down, he kissed the raised tissue and whispered, "I love every part of you, Iris. Battle wounds aren't always physical, but when they are, it's just proof of your brave, brilliant nature."

She glanced over her shoulder, her eyes softer than before. "Antony. I wish we could take our time with this."

He traced the curve of her bottom lip. "Yes, but it's either hurry up or face your dragon. And whilst I look forward to meeting her, I want to claim your human half first. Gives me time to strategize on how to handle your beast."

She smiled. "Then hurry up."

He wanted to slowly take her bra strap down and follow the trail with his lips. But dragons who wanted a frenzy weren't the most patient, from what he'd learned. And even someone as strong as Iris could only control her beast for so long.

So he quickly shed her bra and turned her around. For a beat, his mouth watered at her dark nipples, and he took one into his mouth as his fingers worked on her jeans. Each tug or nibble or swirl of his tongue made Iris arch more into his touch, even digging her nails into his scalp.

Reluctantly, he released her nipple to help her take off her jeans. Once she stood naked, he whispered, "You're so bloody beautiful, love."

Her pupils flashed rapidly again, and she grunted. "Normally, I'd say thank you. But my dragon is impatient, so take off your pants and claim me, Antony. Now."

"As you wish, my dear."

He stripped fast, quite possibly the fastest in his life, and gently lowered Iris onto the bed. She scooted to the top, laid back, and spread her thighs. With her pretty pussy on display, he growled and moved until he could lower between her legs and kiss her mouth again.

She instantly parted her lips, and he dove inside. He loved her taste and took a few seconds to stroke and explore and eventually stopped to gently tug her bottom lip with his teeth. He murmured, "Later, much later, I'm going to take my time." Moving a hand between her thighs, he groaned at how hot and wet and swollen she was. He even thrust a finger inside her, loving how she arched up. "But for now, I'm going to claim my dragonwoman, my true mate, my love."

"Antony, stop being charming and fuck me."

He chuckled, removed his hand, and kissed her quickly. "Just this once, I'll obey without making jokes or teasing you."

She opened her mouth to reply when he positioned his dick and slowly entered her.

Once he was fully inside her, he groaned. "So hot and tight and bloody hell, so perfect."

Iris's pupils flashed rapidly. "Please, Antony. I can't control my dragon too much longer. She wants a turn."

With that, he kissed Iris as he retreated and thrust, increasing his pace as he went. Iris's hands roamed his back, his arse, his arms, and each touch, caress, and light scratch made his cock even harder.

But he refused to come before her. And since he was human, he couldn't make her orgasm with his semen.

So Antony moved a hand and used his thumb to caress her clit in circles, finding the pressure and speed that made her moan and murmur his name with need, until she finally cried out. As her pussy grabbed and released him, Antony let go and stilled, pleasure flooding his body as he spilled inside his dragonwoman.

He collapsed to the side, taking Iris with him. He kissed her, slowly this time, until she finally pulled away. Her pupils flashed, and she said, "It's my dragon's turn. Are you ready?"

Caressing her face, he nodded. "Let's see what she's got."

She smiled. "You might regret those words."

And he watched as her pupils remained slitted, meaning her dragon was now in charge.

Iris had barely finished orgasming before her dragon roared inside her head. *My turn! I want to claim him, to fuck him, until we carry his child.*

I know, dragon. Just remember, he's human and will need more breaks.

Fine. Now I'm done waiting.

Her beast moved to the front of their mind, pushing Iris to the back. Not wanting to be kept inside a mental prison, Iris didn't try to wrestle back control.

She would only do it if her dragon handled Antony too roughly.

Her dragon flipped Antony onto his back before straddling his waist. "Mine. You're mine."

Her male didn't blink twice at how Iris's voice was a little deeper now. He put his hands behind his head and smiled. "All yours, dragon. Claim me."

Iris mentally groaned. The last thing a dragon in a frenzy needed was encouragement or needling.

Although her dragon paused, unsure of how to respond to his reaction. She said, "Do you want me?"

Antony frowned, sat up, and kissed her.

Every lick and nibble and groan wiped away her dragon's uncertainty.

Iris said, *Of course he wants us.*

He always seemed like he only wanted you.

Antony flipped Iris's beast to the bed, on her belly, and raised her arse. He stroked and lightly slapped. "I've heard inner dragons like it this way. So I'm going to claim you, dragon. Now."

As he entered them from behind, her dragon arched into the touch. "Yes. Claim me, human."

As their male took control, moving his hips faster and faster, Iris was amazed yet again. Antony had been able to read her dragon's need and act accordingly.

Somehow, he had done his homework.

But the faster he moved, the less Iris could concentrate. Her beast might have control of their mind, but they both experienced every sensation and the building pressure.

Then he reached a hand around and stroked her clit. Between his fullness from behind and his skilled stroking, the pressure burst and pleasure coursed through their body. Her dragon roared—albeit with a human voice—as Antony stilled and moaned her name.

He remained behind them, curved over their back, and kissed the back of their neck. "Can I take a break with Iris, dragon? This old man needs to regroup."

Her dragon hummed. "For now. But I want you to try and claim me later."

"As in chasing?"

"Yes."

Antony chuckled and kissed their neck again. "I look forward to it, my dear."

Her dragon said, *We're keeping him.*

I agree. Now, let me make sure he rests a bit before we go again.

Aye, fine. But you're going to share equally. I want to see what else he'll do.

Deal.

With that, her beast moved to the back of their mind and Iris took control just as Antony rolled them to the side and onto the bed. Iris moved to face him, her eyes level with his. "My beast said you can have a wee break."

He smiled, stroking back stray hairs from her face. "Good, that gives me time to think of how to surprise her next."

She ran a hand down his chest until she could trace one of his scars. "She thought you didn't want her, for some reason. So, thank you."

He kissed her gently. "I'm still getting to know your second half, but one day, I hope to convince her that I want both of you, all of you, as mine. One day, I'd like to mate you, Iris Mahajan. If you'll have me."

She waited for panic or doubt to set in, but it didn't. No, she couldn't stop smiling at the thought of having this male as her own forever. "Aye, I want to mate you. But I won't officially say yes until after you meet my dad."

He raised an eyebrow. "Do I need to wear my special protective gear, just in case?"

She huffed a laugh. "No, don't be silly. Although, come to think of it, that might impress him. Either that, or if you can find some cricket star to visit Lochguard."

He stroked her hip. "I know a few."

"Of course you do. Who don't you know?"

"Hmm, American football players? Otherwise, I'm fairly well connected. Just wait for your birthday. I'm planning the best party for you, love. Just wait and see."

"I don't need fancy dress or famous people. Just you and our families and lots of food. Which you'll cook, of course."

"I make a mean spaghetti bolognese. I could probably woo royalty away with it."

She rolled her eyes. "Stop being ridiculous."

"Never."

Before she could open her mouth, he rolled Iris onto her back. His cock was already hardening again. "Again? Are you sure? I wanted to give you a break."

"I'm older, not dead, Iris. And I want to claim my dragonwoman again."

And he then proceeded to kiss her and drive her wild and make her come all over again.

He even impressed her dragon, lasting far longer than she'd expected. Until they finally fell asleep before waking to make love over and over again.

Chapter Twenty-Six

Antony lost track of the days. And for a man used to knowing everything, keeping to a tight schedule, and rarely taking holidays, it'd been unsettling at first.

However, he'd enjoyed the breaks Iris's dragon had given him, the "fragile human," as she'd put it. They'd talked and laughed and it'd been like a dream come true, one he'd yearned for but never thought he'd have again after Lisa.

Currently, he was in one of the rest periods, after pleasing her dragon. Iris slept in his arms as he studied her face, and in sleep, she looked younger and more carefree. He definitely needed to spoil and pamper her from time to time. He'd learned the hard way that constantly working could take a toll. Hell, he hadn't realized how tired his soul had been until Iris.

Not wanting to dwell on heavy topics, he debated

tickling her side to wake her up and make her laugh some more. However, his cock hurt and he really should enjoy the break for as long as he could. Dragons were lusty creatures, he'd known that. However, a mate-claim frenzy in real life was more intense than reading about it in any book.

As he thought about his next steps at Wicked Security, Iris eventually scrunched her nose and blinked open her eyes. He kissed her forehead, her nose, and finally took her lips in a slow, lingering kiss. "Good morning, love. I think. It's hard to tell, given how between you and your dragon, you've quite worn this old fellow out."

She rolled her eyes. "You're not old." She stretched her arms and then propped her head on her hand. "And you'd better get used to running on little sleep, because I'm not taking care of our bairn alone. He or she will be a big enough handful as it is, with us as parents."

Before he could reply, she took his hand and placed it over her lower abdomen. As he tried to process everything, she said softly, "You'll be a dad soon, aye? Well, nine months, give or take, but it'll fly by before you know it, as Faye liked to always say."

As he continued to stare, Iris said cautiously, "Antony? Are you okay?"

Her concern snapped him back to the present, and he rolled her onto her back and kissed her. Long and hard, letting her know how happy he was. Eventually, he pulled back to say, "Ecstatic, love. I just, well, for so long I thought I'd never get to be a dad. And once I knew

Max and Lavinia were expecting, it weighed me down a little. But now?" He moved down to kiss her belly. "You're giving me yet another brilliant gift, love."

She smiled at him as she ran her fingers through his hair. "Another one?"

Moving up, he cupped her cheek. "The first one being your love."

As she caressed his back, she said, "Sometimes, I think you're a dream and I'll wake up to find no such male exists."

"No, you're stuck with me, love. For as long as you'll have me. In fact, I want to claim you in front of the clan, if you'll be my mate, my wife, whatever term you want to use?"

She smiled without hesitation, and his heart warmed. "How about partner? And aye, I'll mate you, Antony. And not just because then you can stay on Lochguard permanently. Because knowing you, you'll probably call in a few favors and change the entire process of allowing humans to live on dragon clans."

He winked. "You know I still just might." She chuckled, and he nuzzled her cheek. "How long do we have to wait to mate? Maybe we can see your dad in an hour and have the ceremony as soon as Max and Lavinia can get up here?"

Her lips twitched as she arched an eyebrow. "Where's your legendary patience?"

"In this, nowhere. I want the world to know you're mine."

Her eyes softened, and he added, "I love you, Iris. And I'm impatient to start our family with just the two of us before the little one gets here. And by little one, I mean first a pet and then the baby."

She wrapped her arms around his neck. "A pet, aye?"

"Yes. A pet will be good practice at finding balance in our lives. Plus, you know how much I've always wanted one."

"Aye, I do. And that's a brilliant idea, I think. You can even start a pet portrait collection. Hell, maybe even do it for all the clan."

"Let's take it one step at a time." He kissed her slowly. "I need to have enough time to love my partner as much as she deserves, which will never be enough."

Her voice softened. "You have so much love to give, Antony Holbrook. It's one of the many reasons I love you."

"I love you, too." He kissed her. "So, should we get ready and meet your dad?"

She smiled. "So impatient. But aye, let's get ready. I'm impatient to see how everything went down, whilst we were in the frenzy. The few texts we got didn't reveal much, and I don't like being out of the loop for so long."

"That means we need to shower together, to speed things up."

"Oh, is that the reason?"

"Aye, love, as you'd say. Now, come on. I want to

strut around the clan and show off how I'm the luckiest man in the world."

"Hmm, does that mean we need to get you some peacock feathers?"

"I think that might tickle, if you give my cock a costume."

She snorted. "You never change."

"More like I can be the real me."

And after sharing a lingering kiss with the love of his life, Antony helped Iris shower and indeed strutted around the clan with his dragonwoman, eager to share his life with her. Because he was done living in the shadows now that he'd had a taste of the light, and he was never looking back.

Epilogue

Almost Two Years Later

One of Iris's fraternal twins, Dev, squirmed in her arms, clearly wanting down. However, her lads had learned to walk early and Dev, especially, would find trouble. She couldn't even pawn him off on Antony for a bit since he was a mummy's boy through and through. So she readjusted her grip yet again and murmured, "We're nearly there, Dev. You can play with Alena soon."

"Ley-ley?"

"Aye, your cousin will be there, or so your dad says."

He'd kept the details of their outing secret. It was her birthday, though, and she suspected he'd planned a party.

Antony carried the more easygoing twin, Malcolm, and said, "Yes, Alena and your gran. You want to see Granny, don't you?"

"Gran-gran!"

Iris smiled and ruffled her son's dark hair. "I'm sure she'll have some sweets hidden away, like always."

Malcolm perked up. "Me want."

Antony sighed dramatically. "They are sounding more Scottish than not, aren't they?"

She playfully butted his side. "Aye, and that's not a bad thing."

"Maybe that means I'll have to teach them mimicry. Who knows, maybe they'll follow us into the family trade."

Iris snorted. "And you say I plan too far into the future."

"I think you vastly underestimate our children, my dear. They will be planning escapes before you know it."

"And you'll be encouraging them."

"Hey, you're the one who has a year-by-year plan for self-defense, once they're a bit older."

She readjusted her hold as Dev tried to lean to one side. "I hope they won't need it, but better safe than sorry."

Her dragon spoke up. *We're getting closer to cooperation and peace with dragons from all over the world.*

Aye, but there will always be humans who fear someone different from themselves.

And the best we can do is interact with them more

and more, to try and change their minds by showing who we really are.

You've come a long way from wanting to drop all the dragon haters from the sky.

Her beast sniffed. *I've seen some can change their minds, like that human mated to Zain on Stonefire.*

Zain's mate, Ivy, had once belonged to the Dragon Knights, a dragon hate group separate from the dragon hunters. However, they'd been defeated, which had been one victory, at least.

Iris replied to her dragon, *And there's a wee bit of hope on our side, too. Most of the females we found in that prison have joined the various dragon clans and a few have even mated humans.*

Before her beast could reply, they reached the great hall, and she focused on her mate. "You can just tell me it's a party, aye? Which I don't need. You already gave me brilliant presents this morning, with the portrait of our cats and our lads. I don't need anything else."

He caressed her back with his free hand. "You will always deserve more, Iris."

"I swear, you're going to spoil me too much one day."

"Never, love. The second you look to be going soft, I'll pull strings to get you on a new assignment."

She smiled. Iris had indeed been recruited to Antony's secret department—Wicked Security. Whilst Antony had moved to a more administrative role, Iris helped lead teams from time to time. "See that you do, aye? I'm itching for a new one already."

"If you think I'm going to call off your surprise and do that now, then I'm sorry to disappoint you, love."

"You know I hate surprises, Antony. Can't you just tell me who is inside?"

He winked. "That's no fun. But you'll enjoy the day, I promise. Now, come on."

After being mated to Antony for nearly two years, she'd learned to trust him. Her male would never do anything to intentionally hurt her. Push her boundaries at times? Aye. But not hurt her.

So she followed him into the great hall, down the corridor, and they walked into the massive room used for big celebrations. At first, it looked empty. Then she heard whispering and knew there were people hiding behind the long tables.

However, before she could ask for everyone to come out, they jumped up and yelled, "Happy birthday!"

Even her twins said, "Birfday!"

She took in everyone: her parents; Max and Lavinia; Cooper, Brodie, and their mates; Faye, Grant, and the other Lochguard Protectors; Finn and his family; Scarlett Turner and her mate; some of the people she worked the most with from Antony's Wicked Security team; and even some Protectors from the other clans were there—Kai, Kaine, Robin, Wren, and Killian, with all of their mates.

Everyone she loved or respected was there.

Despite never crying except during her pregnancy, her eyes heated with tears. Iris had come a long way from being on her own, thinking it was the only way she could try to save the world. But these people had taught her differently. Which never would've happened if Antony hadn't burrowed past her walls to show her love could bring you strength instead of weakness.

Antony whispered into her ear, "Happy birthday, Iris." After she met her mate's loving gaze, he caressed her cheek and murmured, "Don't cry, love."

"Mama?" Dev asked.

Looking down at her son, she kissed his nose. "Mummy is fine, I promise. And look, here comes Alena."

"Ley-ley?"

Neither of the boys could quite get out Ah-ley-na, and so they called her Ley-ley.

Max and Lavinia's daughter raced toward them— well, as fast as a two-and-a-half year-old could—with her parents right behind her.

Dev squirmed, and she put him down, just as Antony did the same with Malcolm. The boys had learned to walk early—Antony said it was because they were so clever, although Iris suspected it was more because they wanted to get into trouble—and toddled over.

Alena smiled at her cousins and then beamed up at Iris. "Happy birthday, Auntie Iris!"

Iris was not an easy name for a toddler, which meant Max and Lavinia had helped her practice.

She crouched down, opened her arms, and Alena

rushed into them. Iris replied, "Thank you, Lena." As the wee girl squirmed, Iris released her, and she went back over to Dev and Malcolm. Then she looked up at Max and asked, "Can we play? Please, Daddy?"

While Max was definitely soft for his daughter, he shared a smile with Lavinia before replying, "Yes, but only in the play area over there, okay?"

"Kay!" She took one hand of each of her cousins, and they all watched them toddle over.

Once safely inside the penned area for young children, Max and Lavinia each gave Iris a hug before Antony hauled her to his side. She leaned against him and murmured, "Thank you."

He kissed the top of her head. "It was nothing, love." He whispered into her ear, "I have another very special surprise later, when the lads are asleep."

Lavinia sighed. "Most of the room can probably hear that, Antony."

He winked. "Good."

Iris groaned. "You never change."

"Never, love. You're stuck with me forever."

She lifted her head and cupped Antony's cheek. "Good. Because female dragons are just as possessive of their mates as males, and you're mine."

Antony kissed her. She ignored the whistles and cheers, taking the kiss deeper and showing both her male and the world how much she loved him, incorrigible behavior and all.

Bonus Epilogue

Roughly Nine Years Later

A ntony Holbrook stood inside a hedge maze with Iris, scowling at the nearest wall of twisted branches. He debated crawling through it to the other side and muttered, "I was a bloody spy for decades. I should be able to figure this out."

Iris snorted. "You're just testy because this might be the first time the lads and Lena can beat us to the center."

Every summer, Antony and Iris would visit a new hedge maze with their kids. They'd meet up with Max, Lavinia, and their daughter, and have a contest to see who could solve it first. Originally, it had been the two families against one another. However, this year, the three cousins had decided to compete as their own team since they were ten and eleven years old.

Iris wrapped her arms around his waist from the back and said, "Just stop for a second and assess, aye?"

He turned in her arms and wrapped his arms around his mate. "Hmm, maybe I should take a break. You must be missing my kisses by now."

She rolled her eyes, but her lips twitched. "I'm almost afraid to admit it, but I'll always miss your kisses. But I think we should just stay here for a bit and let the bairns win."

He quirked an eyebrow. "Let them? Are you the same dragonwoman who pushes everyone to their limits when it comes to self-defense training?"

"Only once they're accustomed to the new skills. Next year, we can use all of our knowledge and really make a go of it. But this year? I say let them win. It'll give them confidence and show they can do it. Plus, given how stubborn they all are, if they do lose next year, they'll make plans and strategies about how to win the year after."

"You're brilliant, love. As always."

She smiled. "I'm glad you still realize that."

He laughed before lowering his head. He stopped just shy of kissing his mate. "If we need to stay here and pass some time, then I need a distraction. Do you know of anyone who can help?"

She wrapped her arms around his neck and leaned against them. "Aye, I just might."

Iris pressed her lips against his, and he took it deeper, reveling in her heat and taste. Even after all these years, he never got enough of her.

A group of high-pitched squeals made Iris pull back. "I think they've reached the center. Let's go find them, aye?"

"Are you sure that wasn't Max and Lavinia?"

She raised an eyebrow. "I'm going to mention that to them."

"Go right ahead. Max squeals sometimes. It's a fact."

Snorting, Iris took his hand and tugged. "Come on."

Now that he was more relaxed, Antony easily wound his way through the hedge maze. His sons grinned at him, and Alena did a victory dance. He murmured, "At least we beat Max and Lavinia."

Lavinia's voice came from behind them. "I heard that!"

Before he could reply, the kids swarmed around them and excitedly told them how they'd found the middle so quickly.

And by the time they were all out of the maze, eating ice creams and getting looks for being rather rambunctious, the sun came out from behind a cloud. Antony hugged his mate closer and tried his best to make his family laugh even harder. He'd embraced living in the light, and he was going to make the most of it every day, never taking those he loved for granted.

Author's Note

Thanks for reading Antony and Iris's story! I hope it finally shows how Max wasn't right for her, and how his older brother is more of what she needed. I won't lie—for the longest time I thought Max and Iris would end up together. But as it got closer and closer to when Iris would get her story, it didn't feel right. And for me, if I try to force something, I get stuck. (It's one of the only times I get writer's block, in fact.) So when Antony showed up a few books ago, I knew he was the one for her! And the rest is history.

Also, thanks for your patience in waiting for this book! Not only because last year threw me a loop in my personal life, but it actually took me an extra month to write it compared to my other dragon books. Mostly because I had to go back and find all of these characters (Cooper, Brodie, Trina, Mariana, Alice, Scarlett, etc.)

and make sure their stories wouldn't be inconsistent. (Any mistakes are my fault, of course.) This book sets up the third and final arc of the greater dragon universe, with the dragon hunters. Don't worry, there are a LOT of stories to tackle (I set up six in this book, I think?), but I do have an end goal in mind.

And this isn't the last we see of Wicked Security, either. :) However, the next Lochguard book should be about Brodie MacNeil and Mariana Barlow (she's Emily's mom...Emily is Daisy Chadwick's friend from the short stories, if you remember). Before that, though, will be Dr. Trahern Lewis's story in the Stonefire Dragons series, with his mating of convenience to Grace. He's going to be a tough one, for sure!

As always, I thank not only my readers but also the people who helped to make this book a reality:

- My beta readers Iliana, Sabrina, Ashley, and Amy are all amazing and help the final book shine. Not only do they catch any lingering typos, they also point out the minor inconsistencies I probably would've never noticed myself.

Thanks again for reading! And while waiting for my next dragon book, I hope you'll give my other paranormal romance series, Dark Lords of London, a try. It's a paranormal time travel series with vampires, shifters, and fae witches. The first book is called *Vampire's Modern Bride*. (And my plan is to write the fourth book later in 2025)

Until next time, I'll see you at the end of the next book!

Also by Jessie Donovan

<u>Dark Lords of London</u>

Vampire's Modern Bride (DLL #1)

Vampire's Fae Witch Healer (DLL #2)

Fae Witch's Vampire Guard (DLL #3)

Vampires' Shared Bride (DLL #4 / TBD)

<u>Dragon Clan Gatherings</u>

Summer at Lochguard (DCG #1)

Winter at Stonefire (DCG #2)

<u>Kelderan Runic Warriors</u>

The Conquest (KRW #1)

The Barren (KRW #2)

The Heir (KRW #3)

The Forbidden (KRW #4)

The Hidden (KRW #5)

The Survivor (KRW #6)

<u>Lochguard Highland Dragons</u>

The Dragon's Dilemma (LHD #1)

The Dragon Guardian (LHD #2)

Stonefire Dragons

Blaze of Secrets (AMT #1)

Frozen Desires (AMT #2)

Shadow of Temptation (AMT #3)

Flare of Promise (AMT #4)

Cascade Shifters

Convincing the Cougar (CS #0.5)

Reclaiming the Wolf (CS #1)

Cougar's First Christmas (CS #2)

Resisting the Cougar (CS #3)

Love in Scotland

Crazy Scottish Love (LiS #1)

Chaotic Scottish Wedding (LiS #2)

WRITING AS LIZZIE ENGLAND

(Super sexy contemporary novellas)

Her Fantasy

Holt: The CEO

Callan: The Highlander

Adam: The Duke

Gabe: The Rock Star

About the Author

Jessie Donovan has sold over half a million books, has given away hundreds of thousands more to readers for free, and has even hit the *NY Times* and *USA Today* bestseller lists. She is best known for her dragon-shifter series, but also writes about magic users, aliens, and even has a crazy romantic comedy series set in Scotland. When not reading a book, attempting to tame her yard, or traipsing around some foreign country on a shoestring, she can often be found interacting with her readers on Facebook. She lives near Seattle, where, yes, it rains a lot but it also makes everything green.

Visit her website at: www.JessieDonovan.com